Valens Requested

By: Sherrel Lee

Valens Requested

By: Sherrel Lee

Copyright © 2014

Published at Smashwords

This book is licensed for your personal enjoyment only. This book may not be re-sold or given away to other people. If you would like to share this book with another person, please purchase an additional copy for each recipient. If you're reading this book and did not purchase it, or it was not purchased for your use only, then please purchase your own copy. Thank you for respecting the hard work of this author.

ISBN: ISBN: 978-0-9911733-5-8

Email: Sherrel@sherrellee.com

WEB and Blog: http://sherrellee.com/

Twitter: @gryphoenix

This is a work of fiction. Names, characters, places and incidents are a product of the author's imagination or are used fictitiously and any similarity to actual persons, living or dead, business, establishments, events or locales is entirely unintentional.

Acknowledgement

I owe thanks to Diane, Angela C, Angela H, Jana, Leslie, Steve, Travis, Austin, Max and my editor Lauren. You have all made writing an adventure of a lifetime. Each of you pushed me to make this so much more than I first imagined and I hope the readers recognized the inspiration you provided. Thanks go to my friends at *DARA* who encourage and support this writer's aspirations. And to everyone who takes the time to read the Valens of Legacy Series. Beginning with *Valens Remembered, The Story Begins.* Enjoy reading the stories where the lines between reality - myth, legend and, lore - are blurred.

Contents

Prologue

Bumper-high weeds slapped against the sides of the car as he drove into the middle of the field. He strained through the darkness, to see if anyone was watching. Someone—something—always watched. Knowing that dawn was quickly approaching, he stopped, opened the door and squeezed out from behind the steering wheel. He trudged to the back of the vehicle and flung open the trunk, staring at the lifeless lump of flesh sprawled in its depths. She was the wrong one. It was always the wrong one. Why did the Voice trick him like this? Why didn't it help find and destroy *her*? Instead, he was left to dispose of this putrid, vile abomination. He adjusted his gloves, then dragged it from the trunk, letting it lie where it fell.

A noise drew his eyes to the edge of the field. A copse of trees crouched over the black-green sea, watching his every move. Was IT there? Watching him in the dark? Would it call his name? Lie to him again?

"Dump the trash," the Voice hissed, filling his mind. "Let the sun bake it. Bring the animals to scavenge. Speed the progress of the purification."

Again, he scanned the trees and the field beyond him. Dawn crept closer, over the horizon. *Got to finish. No time. Get the prize. Get out of here. Escape. Hide.*

Are these my thoughts? he wondered. *Or did IT sent them into my brain?*

The body lay at his feet. He took the

hunting knife out of the trunk. Stooping, he picked up the creature's hand, avoiding the long, lacquered fingernails, and stretched out the arm. With one practiced slice, he severed the hand at the wrist. Looking over his shoulder again, rushing to finish before the rising of the sun, he slashed his mark into the flesh that covered its black heart.

Chapter One

Elyna Faylinn, youngest sister to Aiden, Sorcerer King of the Fae, walked through the plantings on Weston's Tree Farm as the sun peeked over the horizon. She loved taking this route to the nursery she managed for her aunt. The Fae were guardians of nature and growing things, and contact with growing plants was more essential to their health than food and drink. Today, she drew comfort from the strong, young saplings. A reminder that there was more to living in the human world than the cruelty and ugliness she had read about in the newspaper this morning. The man the press called the Hand-D Killer had struck again, destroying the life of another young woman and leaving her mutilated body for the police to find.

Distracted by the idea of such unspeakable horror, she stepped into a leaf-covered hole and stumbled, grabbing at a tender sapling to break her fall. It bent, unable to support her weight, and she landed in the dirt, cursing. The young tree burst with sudden growth at her touch, its girth widening, its canopy rising to tower over its companions. Elyna had to scrabble backwards to get out of the way. She suppressed a hysterical laugh, hoping that none of Weston's employees were out this early. How would she explain the sudden appearance of a full-grown tree in the middle of a field of just-planted saplings? Rising, she looked at the stately tree, worrying that other Fae would see what had occurred and realize she was hiding among the humans in Flower Mound, Texas.

Swatting the leaves from her skirt, she hurried on, anxious to remove herself from this evidence of her presence. Using Fae powers to do things that humans viewed as impossible— and leaving the evidence for them to find—was a grave offense, punishable under Fae law. The fact that Elyna's powers were crippled and unpredictable would be no excuse, in her brother's eyes. Now that she had finally created a satisfying life for herself among the humans, she had no desire to draw Aiden's attention. He could still have his loyal subjects drag her back, make her marry Raynard.

Or would he find it a more fitting punishment that her powers had become so useless? It had been over a year since she had lost control this badly. Mainly because it had been more than a year since she had tried to use her powers for more than small magics that any child could do. She, like all her people, was supposed to protect what nature offered, heal the tender life affected by mankind's disregard for the wonders they were destroying. But the curse Aiden had set upon her, for her rebellion, had made her unable to do that. The curse would only be lifted if she returned home and begged Aiden's forgiveness, following his plan for her life. She would rather live without her power than knuckle under to his unreasonable demands— and marry a man she didn't love.

She could still hear Aiden's steely voice as he sat upon the fairy-vine throne and demanded she marry. "You are a princess of this magical realm, sister. You are a subject of this king. You must marry Raynard. You have been promised, and I shall not break our pact."

"I did not make the choice, and it is as much my right to choose as it would be for any other Fae woman."

"You are not *any* Fae woman. You have reached the age of marriage, but who you join with— who becomes your life partner—is *my* choice, Elyna. Mine alone."

She had turned and run to the spring outside the castle. There she could cry, or rail against the truth of his words. She had no rights. She might be forced to mate with Raynard, but the timing for the union would be her decision.

It had been hard to steal away, leaving her family and friends, knowing what it would cost to give up her life and the gifts she'd been born with. The unreliable gifts she now avoided using except to maintain the appearance of a human woman, necessary to deceive those she now associated with.

She caught her hair back and gave it a practiced twist, tucking it into the straw hat she wore. She rubbed her hip. There was going to be a bruise there. *Power of the Realm*, she swore. She had to find a way to regain control of her magic. A mistake in public would bring Aiden's wrath upon her head—and hasten the marriage she'd given everything to avoid.

Moon Flower, Elyna's plant nursery and

shop, sat near the road between Flower Mound and Aubrey, Texas. The area was fast becoming one of the last rural remnants of the county. The land in front of the building had been turned into a gravel-covered parking lot, surrounded by the colorful flowers that were grown in the nursery's greenhouse. The building was a cream-colored backdrop, with forest green gingerbread-trimmed windows. Aunt Faylinn had painted the entry door a night-sky blue, with the nursery's name surrounded by a motif of moonflowers.

Elyna smiled at the cheerful little shop as she stepped out of the trees at the side of the property. She was not surprised to see her assistant Crystal already here, reaching for the extra key in the faux stone that lay among the rock and cactus display next to the back door.

She unlocked the door as Elyna called hello from the edge of the outdoor garden center.

As much as Elyna enjoyed the leisurely walk to work, Crystal loved to tend the plants on the display tables and in the colored pots set about the store before the first customers arrived. "I see you walked to work again," Crystal said as they made their way through the shop to the front door. "I can't believe you enjoy walking in this heat. Why don't you drive the company truck?" She paused, then added, "I know it's not my place to tell you what to do, but with this killer on the loose, it's crazy to walk around alone."

Elyna shrugged off the unpleasantness of the Hand-D Killer. The Fae did not believe in living in fear. "He hasn't struck anywhere near here," she said. "And I enjoy the exercise. When

I leave in the dark, I go around the trees at the edge of the field. A well-worn and very safe path." *My powers, when they work, can keep me safe as well.* "And this morning is cool enough for me."

"Cool, my asters," Crystal said, laughing. "It's already hotter than Hades and the plants are beginning to wilt. You want me to water them?"

"No, I'll do it. You get the change into the cash drawer—it looks like we have an early customer," Elyna said as she glanced out the window and watched a car turn into the parking lot. Taking a moment to make sure her human mask was in place, she adjusted her hat and stepped out the front door to retrieve the hose that hung just outside. Elyna turned on the water, still watching the car.

As the sedan pulled in next to the building, she was surprised to see a bubble light sitting on the dash. That meant the two men in the front seat were cops. Once the car was stopped, they sat inside talking—an argument, to judge by their gestures and body language. After a few minutes, the men exited the car and walked toward her. She peeked out from under the brim of the hat, glad it kept her features shadowed. Some humans could tell there was something unusual about her features, especially in the sunlight, and policemen were often more observant than other humans.

The driver was a young man with a slightly crooked nose, and a light scar that marked his face from his eyebrow to the corner of the eye, stopping at his sculpted cheekbone. *Hot and interesting*, she thought. But looks could be deceiving; she knew that better than most.

She glanced at the passenger. He was an older, heavier man with a large, craggy face. The harsh reality of life was etched into his expression, causing a permanent downward curve of his lips. Surprisingly, a glint of humor danced in his eyes. The way he looked at her made her think he knew at least a part of what she was thinking.

"Dennis," the driver grumbled, "we don't have time for this." He ran his fingers through coal-black hair. "We've got that task force meeting this morning. A killer to catch."

Elyna was startled. "The Hand-D Killer?" she asked. "Has something else happened?"

The older man introduced them. "Hello,

ma'am," he said. "I'm Detective Pratt, and this is Officer Dolan. We're members of the task force working the Hand-D Killer case." He held up a hand. "Now, there's no reason for you to be alarmed—we don't believe you're in danger. But we are speaking to some of the local business owners. The owner of this place around?"

"She's on an extended leave of absence. I'm managing the place for her. I'm Elyna Faylinn. Is there something I can help you with?" Aunt Faylinn had been away for almost as long as Elyna had been in Flower Mound. Elyna didn't expect her to return any time soon. As soon as Elyna had turned up on her doorstep, needing a job and a place to stay, she'd taken the opportunity to go off with her beau on an around-the-world tour.

He gave her a half-smile. "We just wanted to stop in and warn y'all to be on the alert. You're kinda' isolated out here."

"Do you think the killer has been somewhere near here?" Elyna asked. "The paper indicated the last victim was found in the next county."

Detective Pratt took a toothpick from his shirt pocket and chewed on it a moment, studying her. Removing it, he answered, "We had a report from the lady at the crossroad that she saw a car she didn't recognize drivin' around. But I don't think you have to worry. There's nothing to indicate it could be him. We get a lot of calls like that, and they have to be checked out, but they usually don't come to anything. Since we were in the area, though, we wanted to introduce ourselves and warn all the shop owners and so forth to be on the lookout for anything out of the ordinary. Don't hesitate to call, or think you're bothering us. Better safe than sorry."

Elyna studied the officer. She couldn't tell if he really thought the threat was minimal, or if he was simply trying to warn everyone without causing a panic. His face was bland, hard to read.

Officer Dolan's cell phone chirped, and he pulled it from his pocket and glanced at the screen. "Pratt. We've got to go," he said.

Elyna could feel him looking at her, and biting back something else he wanted to say. She could have used her powers to find out what it was, but she tried to avoid invading humans' minds when it wasn't absolutely necessary. "Shi–

Elyna, you and your friend be careful out here. You might want to make sure you have a couple of guys on staff when you're open, until the killer is found. And don't go wandering around alone. Nothing you can do is wasted when it comes to staying safe."

"Of course," she said. They'd obviously gotten some kind of urgent message. A lead? Or another murder? Thank the gods it was no one near here. She watched them get into the car and pull out with a spray of gravel. Shame washed over her. Someone somewhere was suffering, and it was selfish of her to feel relief that she and those she cared for were safe. For now.

* * * *

Dolan pulled the car into the field at the tree line, where another officer stood directing the vehicles to park. The crime scene investigators and the medical examiner pulled up as they got out of their car.

This madman had haunted Gabe for two years. It was because of the Hand-D Killer that he had wanted to join the police force, though no one knew that—not even Pratt. Pratt had pushed for Gabe to be included in the task force, even though he hadn't yet made detective. It took years to earn your shield, but Gabe had other skills to offer—namely, his proven ability to analyze mountains of data and come up with patterns others couldn't see. It just took some persuasion for the detective in charge of the task force to see it that way.

Gabe stopped a few feet away from the victim. This woman was like all the others. She had been young and athletic. Her body was disfigured, her pretty face marked by the torture she'd endured. The killer had left his mark and no other clues.

Pratt joined him. "Devil take him," Gabe muttered. "Do you get used to it? Ever?"

"No, you don't. And you haven't had time to become seasoned. Toughened up. But we need that brain of yours."

Gabe's frustration simmered as he tilted his chin toward the body. "He didn't leave us anything. How does he know to cover all the tracks that would lead us to him?"

"One of these days he'll leave something,

a part of himself. Right now, what we have is only his signature, but he'll make a mistake, Gabe. He'll do something to tell us who he is. We just have to be patient."

"Patient!" Gabe exploded. "He's killed too many. We have to find him. He has to be stopped."

Pratt ignored the outburst and didn't offer words of comfort, turning instead to direct the patrol officers to begin a grid search, working from the roadway and preserving the dump site for the crime scene techs. Gabe observed closely as his mentor had the photographer take pictures of everything, including the tire tracks in the grass, and the way the body lay tossed in an unnatural position. He had the photographer pay particular attention to the left arm, where the hand had been removed, and to the *D* carved between the girl's breasts.

Gabe wondered what the girl had been like. The brief report he had gotten indicated she might have been the one who disappeared from the college campus recently, based on the description. He had a hard time looking at her lying there, naked and disfigured. He'd recently joined the task force and this was only his second body. He couldn't help thinking of them the way they must have been when they were alive. They brought back too many memories. He'd thought he'd be able to look at them clinically, analytically. But this hit too close to home.

Who was missing her? Did she have someone special in her life, or was she a serious student, who studied long hours and didn't participate in the dating scene? What had she dreamed of doing—today, tomorrow, down the road? *Why did you go with him? He only takes those who are alone. You knew there was a killer hunting his prey—why didn't you have someone with you?* Looking up, he noticed Pratt watching him for a moment before turning back to the crime techs.

The day dragged on. Gabe worked alongside Pratt to document the scene, drawing his own set of diagrams as Pratt did the same. He watched as the crime scene team worked, scouring the area for clues, learning how they moved together, but separately. Each person a specialist, requiring little direction as they collected every scrap of debris in the hope it would lead to Hand-D's capture.

When the medical examiner finally finished her exam and ordered the body bagged, Gabe had to move away. The bright blue body bag clashed with the pale corpse, and the thought of the girl being encapsulated in the transport bag unsettled him. Gabe stepped back into the trees and looked out across the field. For a brief moment, instead of seeing the body on the ground, he saw again the woman at the nursery. He wanted to smile at her silly oversized straw hat, and her ankle-length skirt that unsuccessfully masked her slender grace. He had watched her briefly as he started the car, and she walked to the side of the building to water the flowers. The image faded away abruptly as Pratt called him back to the site. There was nothing more they could do. The two men climbed back in their car.

"No time for a break. Got to get back to work." The older man paused a moment, looking at Gabe. "We'll get him, partner. We'll get him and put him away."

Chapter Two

The task force meeting was in full swing when Gabe quietly slipped into his seat at the back of the room. Pratt was talking. "The FBI profiler says we're looking for an older guy. Usually the age of the victim indicates the age of the perp, but this guy is way too experienced and aware of how to clean up after himself. He may be thirties to forties, but let's not limit the field. We also need to determine what the *D* stands for. What it means to our perp."

"Dead, destroy, demented, Dahmer, Dorothy and the Wizard of Oz. Who knows what this crazy has in mind," Riley Hardin from the Sheriff's office sneered. "Until we find him, we won't know."

Laughter filled the room. Gabe still wasn't used to the dark humor the more experienced men used to distance themselves from their emotions. Pratt ended the meeting, and the guys filed out, a few still chuckling.

Gabe walked to the front of the room. "I've got some things to do down the street. I'll be back in about an hour. You're meeting with the Chief?"

"Yeah, lucky me," Pratt drawled. "I get to be the sacrificial goat to the Mayor and Council Member who want a firsthand report."

"Well, good luck, buddy. I can't say I'm sorry to have been left out of that little party." Gabe laughed. "See you later."

Elyna parked the nursery delivery truck at

the curb by the bank. She didn't like to take it through the drive-through—it was too big. She stuffed the deposit bag into her oversized purse, climbed out of the truck and walked toward the bank lobby. She noticed the empty storefront at the end of the walkway had a sign indicating a new shop would open soon. There had been too many empty places in downtown Denton for too long, but the city was working hard to change that. It was amazing what a little fresh paint, some new awnings, and clean streets could do.

"Lady, hand over your bag."

The boy stepped out of the shadows of the empty doorway. Although he was only in his mid-teens, his eyes were irritated and yellowed by disease. His arms were covered by small dots of infection that trailed along his veins, from the needles he must have used. His dark greasy hair hung limply around his acne-pitted face. Glancing at the knife in his hand, Elyna considered her options. She could alter her appearance and frighten him, or use one of her powers to restrain him, then call the police.

"I ain't got all day," he growled. "Give it to me. I ain't gonna ask again." He took a step closer, waving the knife in her face, reaching for the bag dangling from her arm.

The slamming of a car door behind her startled the thief into action. He grabbed her purse, yanking her off balance, and slashed at her with the knife when she tried to catch herself. Elyna fell to the sidewalk, and the boy dashed away around the side of the building.

"Are you all right? No, don't get up.

You're bleeding."

Elyna looked around to see a pair of khaki-clad knees, which bent quickly. Suddenly, she was staring directly into the sapphire-blue eyes of Officer Dolan. The intensity of his gaze was arresting, and her heartbeat quickened. He was holding her hand, gently pressing a snow-white handkerchief against her arm. Heat traveled through her like a tsunami, and she glanced away.

Gabe's brow wrinkled with worry. "We need to get you treatment," he said, looking down at her arm. His words finally penetrated her mesmerized fog.

"I'm fine," she said. "My purse!" She tried to move, and pain shot through her. Her back ached from her hard landing on the cement. Her hand burned from scraping against the rough surface. She looked at her arm again as he briefly lifted the compress to reposition it. Blood welled from a cut where the robber's knife had sliced her.

"I'm afraid we won't catch him," Gabe said, "but he might throw the purse in the garbage down the alley, after he takes your cash. I'll have patrol check and see if they can find it, and at least get your driver's license back."

"I don't need another officer," she said, wishing she could just disappear. The Fae did not attract attention, and people were beginning to congregate, staring at her. Cars slowed to a crawl as the occupants gawked.

Officer Dolan was still staring at her intently, his handsome face concerned. "You're not okay," he said.

That blue gaze was like a magnet, pulling her in. Closing her eyes, Elyna mentally repeated Aiden's mantra: "Fae do not consort with humans, especially those of the opposite sex. It only leads to disaster." Clearing her throat, she asked, "Would you mind helping me up?"

Gabe squinted briefly before his eyes opened wide with surprise. It was the woman from the nursery. "I know you," he said, and immediately felt like an idiot. To cover, he said, "I'm sorry, I don't remember your name." The last wasn't true, but he didn't want her to know she had been on his mind.

"Elyna, Elyna Faylinn. I—my aunt owns Moon Flower." Seeing the puzzled look on his face, she continued, "The nursery you visited with

Detective Pratt." It took several moments before he responded, and she wondered why he had that wicked gleam in his eye.

"Sorry, I didn't recognize the name of the store." His lips quirked into a half-smile at the corner of his mouth. *Or how beautiful you were under that hat*, he thought. "Here, hold this while I call the station." He waited until she put her hand over the cloth before he took out his cell phone and punched in the number.

"I don't want to bother anyone. It's not that important. I mean, he's gone and I doubt we'll catch him now. I'll go find my purse. Really, no need to be dramatic—or protective."

Ignoring her protests, he gave instructions to have a patrol car come to the scene and advised the person on the other end that he would be taking her to the emergency room to have the wound attended to.

Elyna could summon her own healing powers and seal the wound. Leave no evidence the cut had occurred. Instead, she had to remind herself she could *not* use any of the powers of the Fae for her own purposes. They were just too unpredictable. With Aiden's interference curse, a rose garden might grow out of her arm. Even teaching the purse snatcher a lesson would have been borderline. She was living as a *normal* human, most of the time.

As Officer Dolan snapped his phone shut, she said, "I don't want to go to the hospital." She knew it might sound unreasonable to a human, but she couldn't afford to take a chance. Reactions to even the most common drugs were unpredictable for Fae, and could be deadly. It was fortunate that the Fae were not subject to the diseases that affected humans.

He stared at her, eyes narrowing, and she could see he wanted to argue.

"The cut isn't that bad, and I can manage to take care of it myself if you'll just help me up." Her words came out more clipped and rushed than she intended. She could see his jaw clench. "I can get what I need over there. Right across the street. At the pharmacy."

She wished he'd leave, or at least step away, give her some distance. She wondered if he could hear her heart racing. "I really appreciate your concern," she assured him, "but I've got to go. There are things I have to do." She bit back a moan as she tried to push herself off the ground.

Straightening, Gabe reached down and supported her as she stood. She knew her strange behavior made him curious, but a wave of dizziness suddenly had her leaning against him and his arm tightened around her, holding her close. So close she could smell the soap he'd used that morning, and she realized she wanted to put her head on his shoulder and just stay where she was.

.

Gabe could tell when her strength returned and he waited for her to push away, but she didn't—and he had to admit he didn't want her to. She fit perfectly against him, her soft breath on his cheek. Something nagged at him, just out of reach, but he ignored it. *Hanna-bells,* he thought, practicing replacing the curses he had become familiar with in college with less offensive expletives. *She's making me nuts. Who does she think she is, some superwoman, immune to disease?*

The squad car pulled up and the patrol officer joined them. "Search the alley," Gabe said, straightening. Still holding Elyna, he took a half-step back to reassure himself she wasn't going to faint before turning back to the officer. He gave a brief description of the robber, even though he was probably long gone. "Look for Ms. Faylinn's purse—he probably ditched it."

The man jogged down the alley, returning a few moments later carrying Elyna's handbag.

"He dropped it at the end of the alley," he told them. "I'll take it to the station and see if we can get any prints."

"Fine," Gabe said to the officer, "but give Ms. Faylinn her ID. She'll need it when she drives home."

Turning back to Elyna, he said, "I'm afraid we'll have to keep the rest of this for a day or two. I'll let you know when you can come by and pick up anything we don't need."

"Thank you for your help," she said quietly, "and for your concern. I'll take care of the cut, so please don't worry."

He watched as she turned away to walk across the street toward the drugstore. "Elyna— Ms. Faylinn, I'll be glad to help you collect what you need," he said, disappointment rolling through him when she shook her head. As she crossed the street, he watched for the slightest hint she needed help, but there was nothing to justify him racing after her.

In his car, driving back to the station, he found himself still thinking about her. He hadn't felt this angry or protective in a long time. It made no sense. He didn't need the distraction; he had a killer to find.

Chapter Three

The man drove to the field behind the
football stadium and parked among the students'
cars, placing his stolen placard on the dash. The
first time he'd come here, he'd worried someone
would see him and raise an alarm. Even after
he'd gotten a part-time job on the maintenance
crew and could have had a legitimate vehicle ID,
he'd kept using the stolen one, preferring not to
identify the car as his. The Voice had assured
him he would be invisible to the jocks and
lollipops who strolled the grounds, and it had
been right. He could pick and choose—no one
made eye contact, smiled or noticed him at all.

The laughter of two girls drew his attention, briefly. "Wrong, not for me, they won't do," he thought. "Blond is bland." He smiled at that, proud of the lines he had come up with. "Red not dead," he thought, almost laughing. "Don't laugh," he scolded himself. "They'll know I'm here."

As he looked around, he wondered how it was that all these incubators could be so stupid. Not that any female had any brains, but the papers were filled with warnings about the killer. About him. Yet here they were, strolling along like the lollipoppers they were, laughing and carefree. Wouldn't they be surprised if he suddenly just went up to one of them and slit her throat? Her friend would never know what had happened, wouldn't know he had done it because she wouldn't be able to see him. He felt himself getting excited at the thought.

"Fool. Stupid, stupid fool," snarled the Voice inside his head. "Do you believe you are smart enough to do anything without *ME*? You are the left hand. I am the one who tells you when the time is come. When you are *allowed* to choose. *Who* you are to choose."

His hands gripped his head, and he ran back toward the car. He wished he could rip his skull apart, remove the pain of the Voice. He fell across the seat and a cold fist clutched at his heart, squeezing it dry. Lying there, he whimpered and prayed the Voice would release its grip.

"You will bleed for salvation," it spat.

He screamed as his mind filled with

maniacal laughter.

* * * *

Gabe helped Dennis stack and organize the Hand-D Killer files after his meeting with the Mayor and the Chief.

"I ran into Elyna Faylinn while I was out," he said. "She had a run-in with a purse snatcher over at the Town Square Bank."

"Sorry to hear it. She seems like a nice young woman," Dennis said, as he continued returning files to the cabinet. "You got something on your mind? About the lady?"

"I don't know. She seems nice and all, but she didn't act normal."

"Yeah?"

"The perp cut her with his knife, and it

didn't seem to faze her. She didn't even seem too concerned about the theft."

"Maybe she was in shock. You know, it happens when people get attacked. Did she go to the emergency room?"

"No, that's another thing. She acted as if the cut was unimportant. Said she'd take care of it herself. Most people would be worried about infection or scarring."

"Was the cut bad?"

"Bad enough, but not life-threatening. But she ought to have had a couple stitches, probably."

Pratt scratched his head. "She looked pretty solid ta' me. Sure of herself. Maybe she *can* handle it without a doctor. Or maybe she's one of them religious people who don't do doctors." He eyed Gabe shrewdly. "You really worried she acted strange, or is it you finally met someone who gives you that funny feeling in your tummy? You know the one, that feels like its flippin' and doing handstands."

"Are you *nuts*? Where did that come from?"

Dennis laughed. "Boy, it don't hurt if you like this woman. You find her...interesting."

"Don't be ridiculous. I don't have time for this. We've got work to do, remember? Catch a killer."

"Gabe, you don't do anything *but* work. You need a life. A pretty young woman to distract you from time to time might be helpful."

"You're way off base, buddy. The only important thing right now is Hand-D." Gabe's eyes narrowed as he looked at Dennis, who was holding back a laugh. "I'll see you in the morning." He turned and stalked out of the room.

* * * *

The sun was sinking over the horizon as Elyna pulled into the driveway at her house. She had decided to come straight home after the robbery. If Crystal saw the cut, then she definitely wouldn't be able to heal it, even if she decided to risk it—she'd never be able to explain how it had suddenly gone away. She was also afraid Crystal would read something on her face she didn't want to admit. Something about the way Officer Gabe Dolan seemed to sizzle like a steak on the grill. He was hard to ignore, harder to forget.

It would be nice to have someone to talk to about everything that had happened today. She couldn't tell Crystal about making a tree grow ten times its size in an instant, or about being mugged and discovering how Gabe Dolan tugged at her heart. Crystal wouldn't understand why Elyna refused to go to a doctor after being cut by a drug addict's knife. It had been a long time since she had longed for the family and friends she had left behind.

Elyna thought about fixing dinner, but had no appetite. Tried to work on plans for the gardens and landscaping she had contracted to do, but found it difficult to concentrate on anything but Gabe Dolan. He had been so caring and genuinely concerned about her. She could still feel his arms around her, protecting her and holding her—a little closer than necessary? No, she was just imagining what she wanted. A desire that would have dire consequences. He was, after all, human.

Deciding a cup of tea would help settle her, she went to the kitchen, but when she saw her favorite healing stone sitting atop the table, she almost broke down in tears. It couldn't be a coincidence that had delivered this small present at this time. Had Aiden suddenly forgiven her? Known where she was this whole time? Or had she called it to herself without realizing it? Giving up any pretense of calm, Elyna dropped into a chair beside the table, and let the tears fall until there were no more.

* * * *

The following afternoon, as the afternoon temperatures rose into the hundreds, the daily rush of customers quieted and Elyna found the opportunity to do the work she loved the most. Sitting in the potting shed, she moved delicate young plants from the seedling trays to their individual pots, a small act of nurturing that drew her closer to Mother Earth. A knock on the shed door made her glance at her watch. She hadn't realized it was so late.

"Come in," she called, surprised to see Gabriel Dolan walk through the doorway.

"Is there something I can help you with, Officer? Surely you didn't come all the way out here just to say hello."

He didn't answer immediately. Instead, he continued to walk around the room, looking at the variety of flowers and plants sitting on the tables and shelves. "You plant all of these?"

"I like to grow the plants we sell when I can." She watched him, wondering if he was interested or just making small talk.

"Funny." He walked over to the table where she worked. "I never thought about all the flowers you see in shops having to actually be grown by someone."

She didn't answer.

"I'm not much on gardening. You may have already guessed that."

"No, I hadn't thought about it," she answered honestly. It wasn't really a surprise; so few people thought about the plants that were so important to their lives. She wanted to ask how he could be so oblivious, and it made her wonder how she could find him so attractive. Two questions that she couldn't ask.

"I like this stuff." He glanced around at the tables filled with greenery and budding flowers. "I moved into a new house a while back, and so far all I have in my yard is dirt and weeds. I don't have much time since I joined the task force, to think about landscaping. Maybe you can give me some tips on what to do with the yard sometime."

"Is that why you came by, to talk about your yard?" Elyna asked. Had she misjudged him? Maybe he did have more important things to think about than plants, hard as that might be for a Fae to understand. Glancing down at the table, she hesitated to continue moving the seedlings to the larger pots, afraid they would suddenly burst into full growth, or—maybe begin to dance around the room. It was just impossible to tell what might happen with her heart speeding up like a race car as Gabe drew closer.

He sat down next to her and reached around behind him to turn on the fan that sat on the table, locking the rotation so it would stay directly on his back. She grimaced as he noticed her watching him. "Don't know how you tolerate this heat," he said. "Anyway, I thought I'd let you know we caught the guy who stole your purse. Idiot went right back to the same spot where he waited yesterday."

"You found him?"

"Not me—the patrol officer and his partner drove by just in time. He had another woman at knife point—didn't see their car until it was too late."

Elyna sighed with relief, but wondered if she could have prevented the terror the woman must have felt, if she hadn't delayed using her powers on the thief. *At the very least, I could have given him a push and made him fall down*, she thought. *Delayed his escape while Gabe exited his car. He would have been carted off to jail instead of disappearing down the alley.*

"The officers jumped out of their car and charged after him, caught him before he had time to realize what was happening," Gabriel said with a half-smile.

"Is the woman okay?"

"Yeah, she's good. He pushed her down and she got a few bruises. Didn't get cut like you," he said, eyeing the bandage on her arm. "She'll be fine."

Elyna felt uncomfortable as he stared at her, her stomach doing a flip under his intense gaze. She bit her lip. The desire to reach out for him almost overwhelmed her, and the temperature in the greenhouse seemed to be rising higher by the moment.

"Still, I should have done something to stop him, before he preyed on someone else," she said.

"Hey, it's not your fault. You were a victim, too. How is your arm?" He gestured toward the site of the cut. "Are you sure you're not bothered by the heat? Your cheeks are turning red." He grinned, moving closer.

The smile did it. Butterflies dive bombed her stomach. *Wrong. Wrong. I can't feel this way.* She scooted away, feeling more blood rushing to her face, ducking her head so he wouldn't be able to see the desperation in her eyes.

"I'm making you uncomfortable," Gabe said, his voice shifting to on-duty cop. "Sorry. You can come down and get your purse tomorrow if you want. You know the cash is gone, but there were a number of checks left in it."

"Thank you, I will." She tried to think of something else to say. Having him so close was scrambling her brain. "You seem young to be a detective, aren't you?" she asked. Now, why had she brought that up? He'd say it was none of her business. "I mean, I've seen some movies where they are always making an issue of the young officer suddenly making it into the—squad."

Gabe gave a hoot of surprised laughter. "I have special powers," he said.

Elyna raised her eyebrow. Was he Fae or Valen, and she hadn't recognized it? "Powers?"

"I have the ability to see patterns. Make connections the others don't seem to notice, though it hasn't helped a lot yet in finding the Hand-D Killer." He sounded bitter, as if his inability to find the killer was hurting him. "I probably need to go."

Had she offended him? She hadn't meant to. "Why did you really come by?" she blurted out.

He shrugged, not meeting her eyes. "I was in the station when they brought in the perp."

"Perp?"

"The guy who robbed you."

"So you decided to just drive by? I didn't think you had the time to waste on something so minor."

He looked up at her then, his sapphire eyes boring into her. It felt as though he was searching her soul. Looking away, she said, "Telling me about finding the robber is a nice gesture, but you didn't come all the way out here just for that, did you? Why don't you just ask whatever is on your mind. Get it over with."

"Am I that obvious? Thought I had a good poker face." He hesitated briefly. "You aren't like any of the women I've met, and it throws me a bit."

"Is that a good thing or a bad thing?" Did he see past her disguise? Notice her ears looked more like Mr. Spock's than was normal?

"I don't know. You're a puzzle."

"Actually, I'm rather simple. I love to grow

things. I work in a shop that allows me to do what I love. No mystery." Elyna held her breath, waiting for him to say something about the way she looked different. Tell her she looked more like a fairy-tale pixie.

"You didn't react the way I expected when you were robbed. You were all calm and serene, even after you'd been pushed over and cut up by the slimy bast—basket-baller. I wouldn't call you simple."

Elyna sat back, biting her lip to keep from laughing at his unusual curse, grateful he didn't seem to suspect what she was, but suddenly wanting to tell him everything she was forbidden to say.

"You don't cry. Don't ask for help. Instead, you refuse it. You don't even get pale or worried. An idiot cut you with a knife. Most women—most *people*—would be pretty upset about being knifed."

"What can I say?" she asked carefully. "I was alive and basically unharmed, except for my pride. The boy who did this was scared and foolish—that's the reason I got cut." She glanced down at the bandage that covered the wound. "He didn't do it on purpose. The cut looked worse than it was, and I knew there wasn't much to be concerned with."

"See, that's just what I mean. Who is so blasé about getting robbed at knife point?"

What was he really asking? "I'm not sure I understand the question." But maybe she did. Maybe she wasn't acting human enough, and it was making him suspicious. "I was—am—upset,

I just…"

"Your assistant Crystal said you just showed up here one day, out of the blue, and your aunt left a few days later, leaving you in charge. You apparently never talk about your family or anything personal. You come from a family of crooks? Or are you trying to hide from something?"

"No, they aren't crooks." Her laughter rang out at his unexpected conclusion. "What would make you think such a thing?"

"I don't know. It just popped into my head," he said, giving her a crooked smile as he ran his fingers through his hair. He widened his eyes in mock innocence.

Elyna wasn't fooled. He wasn't being funny or silly; he was a cop whose instincts must be very strong, because he really did wonder who and what she was. She wasn't sure how he knew she was something other than what she appeared, but he could be dangerous to her. She found him fascinating, but she was also sure he saw something others didn't: a piece of the real Elyna.

Uncomfortable talking about her background, she hesitated, clearing her throat as she decided what to tell him. "They—my family are just people who live in concert with the land." Looking into his eyes, she saw the doubt. "There's not really much to tell anyone about them."

"So is it just your parents, or do you have brothers and sisters?"

Elyna smiled as she pictured her siblings.

She missed them, and felt angry that Aiden's edict she marry had forced her to leave. "A large family. Eight brothers and sisters."

"Damn. I'm an only child myself. For most of my life."

"Most of your life?" His comment caught her by surprise.

"I was an only child, until my mother remarried when I was thirteen. The man she married had a daughter. We were very close. When they divorced, I lost a sister."

"Oh," Elyna said, biting her lip. "I'm sorry. That must have been very painful."

He looked embarrassed to have revealed so much. "Sorry I mentioned it. It doesn't have anything to do with you." He turned away, picking up a pot at random. "What kind of flower is this?

I don't think I've seen one of these before."

She wanted to ask more about his sister, but Elyna accepted the change of subject. Being around this man was like running at a track meet, and she was having a hard time keeping up. "It's an orchid. I've been trying to develop a new strain. Most orchids are very delicate and need special care, but people love the unusual way they grow, the colors and the texture. Most varieties originally grew in the tope canopies of tropical jungles, and using soil when potting them will suffocate them. They need air even at the roots. I always suggest that they be kept in good light with a soft breeze to circulate the air, from some type of fan. I'm hoping I can find a way to make them a bit more tolerant of household conditions and forgetful caregivers. The ones who don't water often enough or forget to fertilize them regularly."

"It's beautiful, like you," he said, keeping his gaze on the plant, as if looking at her would sear his eyes. Elyna's heart stumbled. Swallowing, hoping her voice would sound normal, all she could say was, "Thank you."

He rose and reached back to turn off the fan. "I have to get back to work. Let me know what time you can come in tomorrow. I'll make arrangements so you can pick up your purse."

Elyna stood and walked with him to the doorway. She told herself she just wanted to go to the office, that it was time to go home, but she knew she really didn't want him to leave. She could have a few more minutes if she walked him to the parking lot, just a few more, even if it was a foolish thing for her to do. The best thing for her would be for this man to walk away and never come back. She couldn't risk taking a chance with a human.

He reached to open the door, but suddenly turned back to face her. His eyes studied her for a moment before he drew her toward him, planting his lips against hers in a deep, greedy kiss. If he hadn't been holding her, she would have slid to the floor. Her stomach grew wings and fluttered, and her heart thundered in her ears. When he finally released her, she swayed, trying to focus her eyes on his face.

"I'll see you tomorrow," he said, walking through the door without another word.

Elyna closed the shed door behind him. Her desire to live the human life even for a brief moment, before Aiden forced her to marry, had been so strong that she had gone ahead without thinking about all the ramifications. For instance, she had never once considered the possibility she would ever become attracted to a human man. She had turned her back on her heritage, but never would she have believed she would consider, even for a second, ignoring the laws that ruled her. Yet she knew, from one kiss, that she might truly break her family's hearts, and cause untold ramifications in the Fae world— because if Gabriel Dolan wanted her to, she just might challenge those laws.

Chapter Four

Elyna sat at the kitchen table with her morning tea, and read the horrifying tale of another woman's disappearance. The woman's husband had returned from a business trip to find his wife gone, and their two-month-old son in his crib, crying from hunger. The news said the police believed the woman had taken out the trash the night before and never returned to the house. Detective Pratt was quoted as saying they were investigating several leads.

Elyna couldn't imagine the horror the family was experiencing, or the sick mind that could take a young mother from her family. She hoped Gabriel and Detective Pratt would be able to find the woman before the child lost his mother forever. Pushing the images of violence from her mind, she rinsed her cup and walked to the nursery.

Glancing at her watch, it seemed impossible to Elyna it was after midnight. After locking up the nursery, she began the walk home. She loved the velvety feel of the night. Stars glistened brightly overhead, and   gauzy film of clouds covered the moon. She liked living in this quiet county, north of Dallas and Fort Worth. The fact that she could walk to and from work held a great deal of satisfaction for her. She didn't live far from the nursery if she cut across the tree farm, where Mr. Weston was still scratching his head over the sudden growth of one of his trees.

As she neared the fields of new plantings, movement drew her vision to the edge of the trees, where something was stirring the tall field grasses. Wondering if it was one of the coyotes that occasionally roamed the area, she stepped quietly through the undergrowth that edged the field, hoping she could see without startling it into running away. Fae loved nature and the creatures of the wild. It was wonderful that coyotes still roamed this developing land.

In the dim moonlight, it took a moment to realize it wasn't a coyote or any other four-legged animal that prowled about. Instead, it appeared to be a person crouched down over what looked like a pile of clothing or—a body. Elyna could just make out a pale arm lying stretched toward the feet of the person who had to be the killer.

Heart hammering in her chest, she slipped closer, trying to see what he looked like, wondering if it was too late for her to help the victim. What could she do? Aiden's curse had made her powers grow unreliable, uncontrollable. She wasn't sure she could call what she might need at will anymore.

She stifled a scream when she realized what he was doing—cutting a hand from the arm of the person on the ground. This was the Hand-D Killer, the man who removed the hand of his victims. Nausea swept over her. Not using the caution to move silently, she darted away, deeper into the shadows.

The killer stopped, looking in her direction. "Who's there?" he bellowed. He stood, searching for her, and then began to run after her.

She fled. *"Cloak,"* she commanded mentally. Nothing happened. She should have immediately blended with the surroundings.

Running, her feet slipped over the slick layers of dead and rotting leaves. She stumbled on fallen branches that seemed to grow taller, thicker, as she struggled to move past them. She fought to stay upright. To move silently. To get far away from the monster who chased her. With pounding heart, she ran.

Brambles and brush reached out, hands bent on tearing her to shreds. Hair, face and clothes caught and snagged. Pain slashed through her as she flew through the undergrowth.

Heart hammering, lungs screaming for air,

she pushed herself forward, struggling to set aside the darkness threatening to engulf her. Calling again for the powers that would unfold her wings.

Stumbling once more, she began to fall. As she spread out her arms to catch herself, gasping for breath, fighting to keep from screaming, she changed. Just as she would have hit the ground, she rose into the air, flying weakly up into the trees. Her body trembled, and she forced herself to clutch the branch she sat on, willing herself to hold on.

The man ran past, cursing and crashing below her. Searching. She prayed the time she had spent ignoring her duties would be forgiven. She heard him change direction, going back toward the field and the body there.

The fairy was almost blind in the night, but as the killer passed beneath her she was determined to follow. She awkwardly slipped from branch to branch, shadowing him at a distance. It felt as though hours had passed, yet it could only have been a few minutes. She saw the shape of him, bent down over the body again, perhaps to retrieve his trophy, and then he ran to a car which sat a short distance away. The engine roared to life and the tires spun in the dirt before they caught purchase and he drove quickly from the field.

Straining from the effort to maintain her wings and balance in the trees, she fluttered down beside the woman lying in the field before tucking her wings away. She gagged as she looked at the damage the killer had done to the young woman, who must have been the mother who had disappeared only two days before. Her left arm ended abruptly in a dark stub. Elyna could see the telltale 'D' cut into the center of her chest.

The woman's body lay exposed to the night, a small pile of clothing at her feet. Elyna felt for a pulse, knowing she would not find it, but unable to dismiss the hope. Knowing there was nothing more she could do, she turned and ran home. As she escaped the terrifying sight, Elyna Faylinn, daughter of the Fae, felt something she had never known before. Fear.

* * * *

Gabriel Dolan and Dennis Pratt were the first to arrive at Elyna's house.

"Stupid! What were you doing, walking

around in this godforsaken place at this time of night?" Gabe yelled.

"I am not stupid." Elyna snapped her mouth closed and stared back.

"I didn't say *you* were stupid. It was a stupid thing to do. Look at you. You're all scratched and bleeding. It's just—never mind. Tell me where you were. Exactly what happened? What you saw."

"It was just a few minutes ago. I was walking home, a shortcut through the tree farm. He was at the edge of the field, crouching over her. I—I saw him cut off her hand."

"What did he look like?" Gabe snapped. Anger was still evident on his face.

"I don't know. It was dark. Big, heavy— stiff when he moved. There wasn't much light. I thought it was a dog or coyote, when I first saw him."

"The car. Do you know the make, model, color—anything?" he snarled.

"Gabe! Give her a break. She's not the suspect." Detective Pratt turned toward her. "Sorry, Miz Faylinn, he kin be a bit of a hothead sometimes. Once he remembers he's working to get his detective shield, he might act a little more professional." Dennis stared meaningfully at his partner.

Gabe drew in a deep breath and let it out slowly. "Sorry. Didn't mean to—are you all right? Do I need to have the medics take a look at you when they get here? *I shouldn't take it out on Elyna. It wasn't her fault that she was there at the same time as the killer. No more her fault than it was when Natalie was killed.*

"I'm fine," she told him tersely.

"Can you show us were the woman is?"

They followed her to the field. Gabe could feel the knots in his neck tighten as they walked. Fate seemed to be toying with him. He had a job to do, and Elyna Faylinn was a major distraction. This woman *would* be the one to discover the victim. He'd sworn, after his moment of weakness in the potting shed, not to have anything else to do with her. He didn't need her involved in this investigation. He owed it to Natalie to find the maniac. That's what he needed to focus on.

Now he was stuck with Elyna Faylinn, the witness. He'd have to see her, talk to her, find out everything she knew. He'd have to see the fright and pain in her eyes as he forced her to re-live the horror again and again in his search for answers.

Reaching the edge of the tree farm, he pushed the too-personal thoughts aside. Looking over the field Elyna had brought them to, Gabe saw the young woman lying pale in a shaft of moonlight. Steeling himself for what he would see, he carefully approached the body and checked for the pulse he knew had been stilled.

"We're gonna' have ta call the forensics team and get some lights out here in this field," Detective Pratt told Elyna, as Gabe barked orders over his cell phone to some poor soul on the other end.

She sat in the dark while the detectives waited for the arrival of their team, thinking about how she'd felt in her small, locked house as she'd waited for the police to arrive. For the first time in her life, the noises outside her house had made her jump and react like a timid child. Tears leaked down her cheeks as she thought about the young woman she had left alone and abandoned in the field.

Her fear had made her angry. Angry that her powers had been almost useless because she thought she knew better than Aiden, her king. Angrier still she'd allowed the monster to escape. She should have done something to stop him. She possessed the skills of a Fae Warrior, but she had barely been able to use her magic.

"Miz Faylinn. Miz Faylinn," Detective Pratt

called, his voice coming closer.

"Over here, Detective," Elyna replied, taking a deep breath to calm herself as he approached. "I'm sorry. I thought you didn't need me."

"No, ya' don't have ta do anything right now, jus wanted ta make sure you're all right. Gabe kinda gave you a hard time and all." He hesitated, watching her, before he continued. "Seein' something like this can't be easy. I don't wanna scare you, but we can't be sure he's not out here somewhere, watchin'. Ya' need ta stay close, where we can see ya', until we can get an officer to take ya' back to your house."

Elyna couldn't think of anything to say. The thought that the murderer might be out there, hidden in the dark or among the trees, was almost more than she could stand right now. She looked around, hating the fear she felt, hating the fact she couldn't tell who or what was near.

* * * *

Dennis looked Elyna over, wondering what she was thinking. He felt sorry for her. He wondered if Gabe had realized how closely Elyna Faylinn fit the description of the victims. Somehow, he thought that was going to be a shock for the boy, who had suddenly become a crazy man around this young woman. *Maybe he does have a thing for her*, he mused. *God help them both*.

He walked back to rejoin his partner, making sure Elyna found a place to wait where they could keep an eye on her. "Gabe, I think we need to talk to the chief 'bout gettin' Miz Faylinn some protection. She's a pretty good match to our victims. If he got a good look at her, she may be in some real trouble," Dennis said cautiously, as he rejoined his partner.

Gabe felt his chest suddenly tighten. He looked over at Elyna, who was pushing strands of chestnut hair from her face.

He couldn't believe he'd never once thought about how much she looked like the victims. How similar her looks were to Natalie. Dennis's words drew his mind back over the last few days. What else had he missed? Was that the reason he'd felt like shielding her from the world? He'd lost Natalie. Was it the fear of losing this woman that was making him so crazy, and he hadn't even realized it? Scowling, he turned his back. He didn't have time for the fear he felt for

Elyna Faylinn.

He was thankful when one of the techs called out to him. "Killer was sloppy tonight, maybe because of your witness. Left us a little treasure." The man lifted an evidence bag that contained a blood-smeared hunting knife. "Must have left in a hurry."

Gabe felt Elyna approach and turned to see what had drawn her. She cringed as the search team began to set up the lights and take pictures. Her face told him what she was thinking. He could almost hear her revulsion at the stark exposure. Her desire to run to the victim and cover her body. He understood the feeling much too well.

On the other side of the field, the killer

crouched, watching the police. He could see the woman at the edge of the trees where he had heard her before he had run away.

"Fool," the Voice snapped. "You left all for them to find. You will be discovered. They will know you. Know what you have done. You are unworthy, just as I have always believed."

The killer clung desperately to the limb of the tree where he had concealed himself, fighting to think as the Voice pummeled him. "Incompetent, ignorant, you are nothing. You must find the one who is chosen to be destroyed."

Aiden, King of the Fae, lounged on the Throne of Benevolence, listening to the requests of his subjects. The room was filled with members of the court, as well as those who wished some boon from him. A soft buzz of conversation filled the room, as those present talked among themselves. Normally he enjoyed this time, meeting his subjects, granting favors, but it was hard to concentrate today. Corwenna, his wife's handmaiden, was droning on about something. He didn't know why his wife didn't just grant the child her wish, as she could have done. Instead, he had to listen to every nuance of the words to determine what the girl actually sought.

Tension hardened his muscles. He straightened, abruptly signaling Corwenna to silence. The errant wind carried a disturbing echo. Elyna! He felt suffocating fear, and then a sadness so intense it almost swept away his ability to think. He wanted to be angry that she had contacted him, but he realized almost at once that her emotions were so strong, she didn't realize she was reaching out. It had been so difficult not to send his guards after her, when she had left so suddenly. But despite what Elyna believed, he wasn't an ogre, and could understand his wildling sister needed time to come to terms with her destiny.

He missed her, but had not intruded in her mind, allowing her to remain lost to him. He had known, through his gift of sensing the future, that Elyna had a dark and lonely destiny to travel before she would be ready to accept her responsibilities to her people. Foolishly, in his desire to protect her, he had tried to circumvent that by arranging a marriage for her—but he of all people should have known that fate could not be denied. He opened his mind to his sister, letting her thoughts and fear move through him, feeling the pain of discovering a savage killer. The despair of having left her family and friends, and facing this horror alone.

This, then, was her time of crisis. His emotions warred with his duty as king of the Fae. He could not walk Elyna's path for her, nor could he send more of his people to interfere in the affairs of humankind. Fae guarded and protected the natural world; it was not up to them to rule the creatures in it—nor to save them from their own folly.

But he could send his sister help and protection—if he were careful. In her mind, he had seen their aunt's shop, and knew who could go to Elyna, know who and what she was, and watch over her. The Phoenix. Leader of the Valens, who owed him for having supported her cause to eliminate the creatures created by Cerberus.

He knew from experience that Jemma Nix—the Phoenix—had not yet developed her mental powers to the point that he could contact her mind directly. No matter. Aiden had an emissary already among the Valens—a trusted servant. Mai Tallrock could be his liaison with the Phoenix, as always. And perhaps it would not be too much interference if he asked Mai to visit Elyna herself, to pave the way for Jemma. To see for herself if his sister was truly all right.

.

Chapter Five

Elyna unlocked the door to her house and dropped onto the couch, exhausted. She had felt waves of sorrow coming from Gabe as he drove her home. Now he was checking each room of the house, insisting on making sure no one was here before he would leave her.

She looked at him as he returned to the living room. He looked tired, with bags under his eyes, and she saw sadness in them that normally didn't show on his face. It made her want to reach out, run her fingers over the scar along his eye. Use just a little magic to ease the pain and chase away the darkness that hovered over him.

Stopping in front of her, he took a deep breath and let it out slowly before he said, "You may be in danger."

"Why? He didn't get any better look at me than I got of him. I was in the shadow of the trees, so it would have been hard for him to tell what I looked like."

"You weren't in a car. He'll know you have to be from around here."

"Maybe." She rubbed her arms, dagger claws creeping up her spine.

"Don't underestimate him. He's a killer, but he's smart," Gabe said, and walked to the door. "Stay alert when you return to the nursery. I—we—want you to stay safe."

"Is my safety so important to you?" Elyna

asked before he could open the door.

He hesitated, turning back to look at her. "I don't want it to be. I mean, I don't want it to be that personal—but yes, *I* want you safe. You've stirred something within me I haven't believed I could feel again—never wanted to feel again. The need to shield you from harm."

"Why me?"

He shook his head, unable to explain what he felt. Unable to talk about Natalie.

She didn't think she would be able to sleep, but after a soak in the bathtub, she lay down on her bed and stared at the ceiling. Gabe Dolan's face seemed to stare back at her. The look in his eyes before he left had opened a new wound in her heart. She wanted to know his secret, ease the pain, but even if her powers were fully predictable, she couldn't invade his mind in that manner. If he discovered her abilities, he would never understand, and she would never be able to explain.

She couldn't believe she was falling for a human. What would Aiden say if he knew? Would he shun her? Demand she never return to the Fae lands? Worse, would he place her in a tower for hundreds of years and allow Gabe to fade from memory when he died, as all humans did?

* * * *

She was glad to be back at Moon Flower. Even one day off to rest seemed too much, and she had spent most of the time away dreaming of being alone with Detective Gabriel Dolan. She went directly to the greenhouse because she needed to press her hands into the soil and tend the new plants. When Crystal appeared at the door, Elyna said, "Now that we know the Hand-D Killer has been in this area, you need to be careful. No working after hours for a while. No coming in before daylight. No working alone."

"Does that go for you as well? I'm not his type, but you are." Crystal wrapped her arms around herself. "Women with long brown hair, slender, athletic—that's you. The super-outdoorsy sort. You're the one who could get into real trouble. Makes me feel sick to think about it."

Elyna suddenly felt her head swim. She knew she was sitting in the greenhouse. A part of her could see the seedlings, yet she was also in a room she didn't recognize. It was small and dark, lit only by candles sitting on a table filled with crosses of all shapes and sizes.

She felt a rising terror as a voice chanted in the background. At first she couldn't make out the words—the thunder of a heartbeat roared in her ears. She felt small, like a child, and the dimensions of those things around her seemed to bear that out. The chanting grew louder, and the voice came closer.

"The left hand must bleed to reach salvation." The words were repeated again and again. She trembled, knowing the voice would come closer. She felt hot, fiery pain as something sharp slashed into her body. Her back. Her arms.

"Elyna! Are you all right? You're white as a ghost. You going to faint?" Gabe's voice slashed through the vision as he pulled her into his arms.

Shaking her head, trying to vanquish the images that lingered, she looked up into his face, seeing Crystal standing over his shoulder. Worry was written across both their faces.

"Where did you come from? What happened? I must have been daydreaming or something."

"Whatever it was, that wasn't a daydream," he said. Embarrassed he had acted so rashly, he dropped his arms and took a step back. "You need to go home, get some rest. I'll drive you—"

"I'm all right." But she wasn't, and she wished he hadn't moved away so quickly. She didn't have visions unless it was the mind of a friend or family member, opening to share something with her. How had this happened?

"Your stubborn is showing, Elyna," he said with a quirk of his lips. "Really, you've had a major shock, and came back to work too quickly."

She shook her head again, opening her mouth to speak, but Gabe went on. "Don't go trying to tell me it hasn't affected you. Anyone would be having nightmares over what you found. I don't imagine you've slept too well."

"Maybe you're right. I do feel a little strange," she conceded.

* * * *

The man slowed down when he saw the unmarked car turn out of the drive, heading toward him. Probably just some grunt out asking questions. Police were so stupid. They seemed to think no one could recognize their cars. They never solved anything important. He almost

drove into the ditch when the car passed him and

he realized *she* was sitting in the front seat with

the officer. She had been hiding from him, but

he'd found her. Now all he had to do was work

out a plan to come back when no one was

around. Follow Dorothy home. Send her to hell.

* * * *

Thick drops of rain fell as Elyna got out of

Gabe's car in front of her house. Within the time

it took to take the few steps to get inside, the

floodgates opened to a typical Texas

thunderstorm. Lightning brightened the sky and

streaked in majestic jagged displays to the

ground. Thunder rolled across the heavens,

rattling the windows.

Gabe refused to leave, but suggested that

Elyna try to rest. Sleep wouldn't come. The voice, followed by the vision or whatever it was, had been too disturbing.

The thunder roared, so close she could feel it in her bones. She sat up, watching through her bedroom window as the wind blew and twisted the trees. A sound coming from the kitchen roused her; she recognized it as the kitchen cabinet doors opening and shutting. Thinking it might be Gabe searching for something to eat, she rose and walked down the hall.

She found him sitting with a magazine on his lap, staring at the open page with unseeing eyes. He was suspended in time. A feat only a very powerful Fae could perform.

"*Mai*," Elyna gasped, staring at her

brother's faithful servant. Mai Tallrock stood in her kitchen making tea, dressed in blue jeans and a snug-fitting t-shirt that displayed her hourglass figure to perfection. Never had she seen Mai in such casual clothes—but then, she hadn't seen her since she left to join the Valens of Legacy.

"I thought we could use a warm drink, and I love these special teas. I rarely drink it at home, but it's such a treat when I am traveling."

"Of course, Mai, but as you are my brother's personal envoy, I should prepare it for you. Would you like something to eat?" *What on earth had brought her here? Had she come to take Elyna back to Ireland*? Elyna felt awkward. The earth seemed to shift just a little at the thought of Aiden's anger.

"Oh, sit down, child. I'm perfectly capable

of fixing the tea and raiding your cupboards." Mai gazed at her appraisingly. "Much has happened of late; you are confused."

Elyna didn't know how to respond. How much did Mai know? How much should Elyna confide in her?

Mai bent down and retrieved a baking tray from the lower cabinet, flipping her raven hair out of her face. Her movements were quick and efficient. "I hope you don't mind, I have helped myself. I needed to let you know you will have a visitor soon, and are to welcome her as though she is expected. The human policeman doesn't need to know you've never met. Aiden has sent her, and her quest is to return you home after the killer who threatens you is captured."

Stunned, Elyna nodded as though she

understood.

"I can see the darkness emanating from you," Mai said. "Finding a woman dead in a field is disturbing, but there is something else with a hold on you. Aiden feels you must play your part for the humans, in the capture and punishment of this madman. When that has come to completion, we will return home so you can take up your duties as a princess of the Fae."

"Is Aiden angry with me?" Elyna asked, staring into the dark chocolate eyes of the woman standing in her kitchen. Did Aiden intend to punish her? Would she need to run again? How could she return home now, without knowing what Gabe felt for her, or she for him?

"He loves you, Elyna, and surprisingly, he feels he understands why you needed to leave, but he is also your king and you must obey him, or the consequences will be much more dire than his curtailing your powers. Now, I will tell you what I can. However, I must ask: has life treated you so badly you turn your back on the very core of who you are? No matter how hard you try to ignore it, you are of the Fae. Running away will not change that."

Elyna shook her head, and watched as Mai brought fresh shortbread and tea to the table. "It's not a matter of being treated badly. But humans—in this country, at least—have so much freedom to choose their own paths. I wanted to experience that freedom."

Mai studied her for a moment. "Freedom benefits only the self; duty benefits all the Fae, and the world." When Elyna said nothing, she went on, "Enough about that. Now, tell me what happened."

"It's more than just the woman who died. I had a...I would say a vision, this afternoon."

"The Fae often have visions. We see the thoughts of our friends and family. Perhaps you were feeling the concern Our King has, that you have left your home."

"No," Elyna said, shaking her head. "This wasn't family or friend. This—I think I saw the visions of a human. The killer."

Mai set her cup down and stared at Elyna, concern clouding her eyes. "Human. That is not a gift we are known to have. You believe this? There is no mistake?"

"I was talking to one of the people I work with. My mind was filled with the vision, though I knew I was still in the greenhouse. There was pain and fear. A sinister voice that chanted. No, I've not made a mistake. The vision came upon me from a human source. A very dangerous human source."

Mai stared at her. "This connection that has come upon you is very dangerous. Without your full power to protect you, it could kill you."

"Kill me? I don't understand. I never heard of a Fae capable of reading a human." The storm raged more fiercely outside the small house. Elyna wondered if Mai was the cause. It was well known the Fae of the king's court could control the skies, and often brought on violent weather when angry.

"You must take this warning to heart," Mai said abruptly. "And Elyna, you must not involve yourself with any human. Connecting with them in this way would be dangerous to you both. This power should be shared only with the one who will complete you—you must mate within the Fae. There are those in the world who would do anything to have control over such a power—the knowledge of the past, and of the mind of a human. Unfortunately, we know that greed and hatred are not limited to the human race. Knowledge that you have this ability could cause irreparable harm to Fae and Mankind."

"I know well the law of the Fae," Elyna said quietly, though anger rose like bubbles in a boiling pot. "I have been well-schooled as a member of our royal family."

"Of course, Princess. I did not mean to offend." Mai rose to leave. "Your guardian in the other room will become aware again soon, and soon after that, Jemma Nix of the Valens will arrive. King Aiden has told me there is a time of darkness coming to you. You will be sorely tested and will have to call upon all the gifts you have been granted. He loves you, but as king he must work through others to help you, and he has called upon the Phoenix to serve in this regard. Take care, Elyna. No one wants to see you hurt."

Mai disappeared as Gabe called out from the couch, "Sorry, I must have dozed off. Did you get some rest?" He walked into the kitchen and snatched a cookie from the plate that still sat next to the pot of tea.

Elyna was reaching into the cabinet for cups, and set one down in front of him. "Yes, I rested. Have some tea, then you can go back to work. I know you didn't intend to babysit me all afternoon, and I'm expecting a friend of the family in just a bit."

"You didn't mention him—her—on the way here. Who is it?"

Elyna couldn't suppress the laughter that bubbled up at the look on Gabe's face. "Are you asking as a friend or as a detective, *Mr.* Dolan?"

Gabe gave a wry smile and shrugged. "Can it be both? Hazard of the job, I guess. I question everything."

"*Her* name is Jemma Nix, and she owns—"

"Legacy Security," Gabe said, with a downturn of his lips. "Did you call her? Ask for her to send protection? You know I—the department will make sure you stay safe. I'd think you would trust me to protect you rather than calling some hotshot private security firm."

"I didn't call them, but I don't know why you'd have a problem if I did. You're the one who's always telling me I'm not being careful enough, and now you're accusing me of some hidden agenda. It just so happens that Jemma is a friend of my brother's." Elyna pushed down her anger, determined not to overreact to the swings in emotion Gabe displayed. "These killings have made national news. You can't blame him if he asked her to check up on me."

Gabe's face said he didn't believe that was all there was to it, but he didn't challenge her either. He just excused himself and left before Jemma Nix arrived.

Chapter Six

Gabe leaned against the porch rail outside the nursery office, tired and worn. As usual, his hair was rumpled and stood on end. Two days had passed without a solid reason to check on Elyna. Since he had been assigned to attend the Hand-D task force meeting with the Denton Sherriff earlier, he had decided to stop by. He knocked harder on the door, hoping Elyna would be the one to answer it, and that she checked to see who it was before she did so.

The door opened.

"You didn't check to see who it was," he said. "I hope I don't have to remind you—"

Elyna said, "Yes, Officer Dolan, but I thought we had finally got past you being Mr. Bodyguard after you slammed out the door when I was expecting Jemma. I saw your car when you drove in. I had to finish putting the receipts away before I was able to answer your knock."

"Oh." He gave her a sheepish smile. "I told you I care about you, didn't I, and I try to guard my—friends from harm. Can we call a truce tonight? I thought maybe, if you haven't had dinner yet, we'd drive into town and get a bite to eat. Unless, of course, you have plans with Ms. Legacy Nix."

Surprised at this sudden offer, she said cautiously, "No plans. Jemma has a training facility not far from here and went to work out, but I'm not really dressed to go anywhere." Elyna looked down at her pants, dusting them off.

"I know a place where no one will notice. Do you want to go or not?"

Suspicious, she hesitated before answering. "I need get my purse," she said, sure he was going to say something snide.

"Look. I owe you an apology. I know I've been acting like an ass—ter. I'm hoping to make up for it, and dinner seemed like a place to start." Gabriel walked ahead and opened the car door, and waited for her to finish locking the shop

They talked while he drove to Carrollton, turning often until she was lost. She hadn't been paying much attention to where they were going, so she was surprised to realize they were pulling into the drive of a very large house in a newer subdivision.

"This doesn't look much like a restaurant to me," she said, puzzled and a little uneasy. She had dreamed of being alone with him, but it scared her a little. She wasn't sure what he would expect or what she would do if things got—heavy.

"I never said we were going to a restaurant. This is my place. Thought we could talk. I can rustle something up in the kitchen—I'm pretty sure I have groceries."

They walked through the barren family room into a raised kitchen area. The entire back wall of the great room was filled with windows and French doors opening onto a patio and large yard filled with—as he had promised—dirt. A brick wall rose up to hold the dirt in. "How long did you say you've been living here?" Elyna asked, looking at the yard again.

"Not quite a year. If I remember correctly, I did tell you I needed a landscaper."

He stuck his head into the refrigerator and began to collect food and place it on the countertop.

She watched him as he chopped, sliced and started everything cooking. It was obvious he was at home in the kitchen, and from the way her mouth watered, she was sure she was in for a treat. They talked about families, friends, and everything else they could think of as he worked on the meal.

"It smells wonderful. Where did you learn to cook like this?"

"I was lucky. My mother has a chef and he took pity on me. Decided every man should be able to cook. Said it would impress people."

A chef? Was Gabe rich? Was this the house a rich guy would buy? Why had he become a cop if his family could afford a chef? She looked around more carefully. "I have to admit, I'm impressed."

As they ate, questions tumbled through her mind. There was something sexy about a man in body-hugging blue jeans and a black t-shirt who could handle himself so well in the kitchen. And she hadn't forgotten the afternoon in the greenhouse at the shop when he had suddenly kissed her. Would he kiss her again? He had offered her dinner and brought her to his house; did this mean he intended to try to talk her into his bed? Mai's caution against involvement with humans refused to be dismissed, but the tingle of excitement at doing something irresponsible sent a shiver dancing along her spine. "I like your kitchen," she said, trying to distract herself from the wicked thoughts.

"Don't really know what to do with the rest of the place."

"Then why did you buy it?"

"I didn't. I have a mother with guilt issues. She marries and divorces rich men like they were collectibles. She abandons me, then has issues with the guilt it causes her when she remembers she has a son."

Elyna wanted to laugh and cry. "Gabe, I'm so sorry. I admit, I wondered how a police officer—a young police officer—could afford a place like this."

"I am young, but being on my own gave me the drive to grow up faster, and it didn't hurt I have an I.Q. better than most. It caused quite a stir when the Chief gave me a temporary spot on the detective squad. On the other hand, being the youngest has some perks. Everyone outside the force underestimates me. And unfortunately, that brings us to the reason I asked you here this evening."

"The reason? I thought you were asking me out. Like a date? For dinner?"

He looked a bit embarrassed. "Sorry. It wouldn't be ethical to ask a witness out on a date."

Elyna's face flushed scarlet. Heat traveled through her entire body as humiliation turned to insult. "You didn't have to play a game, Officer Dolan. You could have given me the courtesy of stating your true reason for the invitation. I'm not a child who needs to be coddled."

"Elyna, I didn't mean to—"

"So what is this important thing we have to discuss?"

Gabe let out a sigh. "The department is having budget issues and discontinuing the extra patrols in your area. I was hoping to convince you to take a vacation. Get away until we catch this guy."

"That's ridiculous. I'm responsible for running my aunt's nursery. There are employees that need to be paid. I can't just close up and disappear."

"Yes, but—"

"I need to leave. I won't have this conversation right now." Elyna snatched up her purse and headed for the door, ducking her head so he couldn't see the hurt in her eyes. She felt like such a fool, thinking he was interested in her as a woman. And telling him she thought this was a date!

"What are you going to do? Sprout wings and fly away? I'll take you home," he said, snatching his keys from the entry table.

Releasing her wings and flying home wasn't an option this early in the evening. Too many people might see her, and that was definitely something she had to avoid. Instead, she had to accept the ride.

A single word could have set off a firestorm as he drove her back to her house.

When he dropped her at the front door, he couldn't hold back another warning. "Natalie, you're being foolish. I want to protect you."

Elyna blinked. Who was Natalie? But she had no chance to ask before he drove away.

* * * *

If there were gods of chaos, they ruled Gabe's life. Only a few hours after the horrible trip to take Elyna home, he had ended up at her door again. Now she sat in his car, in the parking lot of what had been the nursery, the wet, acrid scent of burned wood filling the air. Someone had torched her greenhouse.

The lot was filled with emergency vehicles. "Stay here," he said. "Only official personnel should be walking around here until we're sure there's no danger." He got out of the car.

She didn't argue, just stared out the windshield at the frenzy of activity around the shop. Gabe could see the shock on her face, and he wanted to take her in his arms, shield her from the sight of the fire still raging in the greenhouse. Let her bury her face on his shoulder. Cry out the grief at the loss of the beautiful plants and trees that she had tended with such care.

It took hours to get it under control. Men slumped in exhaustion from the heat of the last flames as they fought back in the hot, humid June night.

He had checked back with her through the long night, tried to get her to leave, but she wouldn't. He'd taken the arson investigator over and introduced him, but beyond that, there was nothing he could do for her. Except find the person responsible for this ruin.

"The offices in the back are gone," the investigator said when he joined Gabe, who was talking to the captain of the crime scene techs. "We were able to save the shop area, but it might have been better for everyone if it had gone up in smoke as well. The SOB who did this…well, I'll leave that for you to see."

Gabe walked back to the car. It seemed like days since he'd left her there, but in reality it had been only a few hours. The crime scene techs were loading up their gear. They had completed collecting the samples and evidence.

"I want to see it," she said. "I want to see the shop. Can you take me in?" She closed her eyes, trying to see into the future. See what would come out of the rubble. Instead, all she saw was the destruction. She pushed down her rage. A sudden and violent storm, touched off by the tumultuous emotions within her, would benefit no one, and she wasn't sure she could keep the lightning from striking those who had worked so hard through the night.

"It's going to be painful, seeing what he did."

"Who? I don't think I know anyone who hates me or my aunt this much." She was suddenly inside his head, feeling the anger he was experiencing. The sorrow for her suffering. The determination to find the man who had hurt her. She gasped, knowing she had violated him, yet finding it difficult to pull away.

"Elyna, it was Hand-D. He found you, and

he wants you to know. He carved that letter everywhere." His words vibrated with rage as he opened the car door and escorted her to what was left of the shop.

She hesitated when she saw the blackened remains of the cashier stand, the plants shriveled and curled from the intense heat that must have raged through the room. The man had committed another form of murder, torching the Moon Flower, and her heart broke as she thought of the care Aunt Faylinn had taken to create a place of respect for nature. Taking a deep breath, she followed Gabe into the room.

He showed her the gaping wounds left by the knife; its owner had slashed "D's" into the walls and the counter.

"What happens next?"

"I do everything in my power to protect you. And you do everything in your power to stay away from him," he told her sincerely.

"That sounds simple enough." *Stay away? Not likely, but I will do everything in my power to help you find him and destroy him*, she promised silently.

Gabe watched helplessly while tears gathered in her eyes. Her fight to hold them back was unsuccessful. This time he didn't hesitate, reaching out to hold her close, comforting her, and trying to hide the fear that the madman would find her

* * * *

Jemma morphed from Phoenix form and walked through the destruction left by efforts to fight the fire, and by the killer who had declared his challenge to Elyna. Would he have done so if

he had known who and what she was? Or was

he too desperate in his quest to kill his own

demons to care? Elyna had told her of her vision.

The time she had spent inside the killer's mind.

Jemma worried about what she had

glimpsed in Elyna's mind before shutting down

the connection. The girl the humans thought was

a woman, forced to hide her true nature. Gabriel

was far more experienced in the human world—

with his mental acuity and the years of schooling,

he had experience to equal those older than he,

but he was perhaps not as wise. Would Gabe

reject Elyna when he found out she was not

human? But this was not why she was here, she

thought, setting those concerns aside. She

needed to focus on helping to catch a killer. A

madman who destroyed more than the lives he took.

Aiden had been clear—she must not let anyone know Elyna was his sister, even other Valens. In her opinion, a ridiculous ban, made only to protect his powerful image. It there was anything Jemma had learned from Hawke, being able to show how much you cared not only made you appear stronger, but gave you strength. But she would honor his request when she called upon her trackers to find the scent of the man the humans were calling Hand-D.

Mentally she called to Gage Wang, black dog tracker. He was in Flower Mound for a meeting with Griffin Hawke, and could be spared from those meetings for an hour or so. She didn't expect him to track the killer, who was in a car, but she was hoping Gage, so sensitive to scents, would be able to give her some other clues that might help her to determine where the madman was hiding.

Gage arrived twenty minutes later, having been at the training facility only a few miles away. Before transforming from his Tiangou form, he took time to seek out the scents that the murderer had left behind. He had to sift through the smells left by the fire and police personnel, the most recent customers and the workers who had been in the building at various times, but it didn't take long to find the odor of hatred and desperation. "The man you seek is out of control," Gage said as he joined Jemma in the center of the shop. "There is the stench of death—many deaths— upon him, but the people here are strong, including the Fae who walks among them. They will be able to overcome the madness if he comes near them."

Jemma ignored the reference to the Fae, and Gage didn't challenge her. "Do you find anything to help locate him? Anything unusual?"

"Perhaps. He carries the scent of many who are young, which could mean he has a job in a building where many students roam the hallways. A janitor or maintenance man, someone who does not come in direct contact with them but walks among them regularly. I would say he lives somewhere hidden as well, perhaps with the bodies of his prey. That odor of death is deep and permeates his movements. Humans may find him distasteful when he is near."

"I will be sure to pass your findings to the detectives. Before you return to Hawke, I have two more assignments. Find the killer's trail, and follow it back to the location where he parked his vehicle while he destroyed this site. Maybe you will be able to parse out some other clue about where he hides." She handed him a slip of paper. "Then, go past this residence to determine if he has been there. I'm sure I don't need to tell you, this is not to be discussed with anyone else. Even Hawke must remain uninformed at this time."

Gage gave a nod, morphed back to black dog, and began to follow the trail the killer had left. He would report back any findings though the mental link they shared.

Jemma prepared to meet with the

detectives who were seeking Hand-D. They

would not be pleased to see her, but they would

want the information she could provide.

Chapter Seven

Elyna finally understood what Crystal meant about feeling butterflies in her stomach. Gabe had called and invited her to dinner, promising to take her to a restaurant this time, to talk about anything but the recent events they found themselves entangled in. A real date, or just a duty because he was feeling protective? But she knew it wasn't the job; she had felt the tug-of-war within him when she had read his mind. He was afraid to love, but that fight was already lost.

She'd never been on a date, and he had tried to pretend this wasn't one, to make the invitation have an official sound. He was still fighting his own emotions. Still, she couldn't hold down the excitement she felt at the idea of seeing him. She dithered—what should she wear? Should she introduce the subject of the Fae? How could she do that without breaking the laws of her race? Or making him think she was crazy?

A knock at the front door announced Jemma's arrival. "I wanted to tell you what we've found at the nursery, and to offer you the protection of my home while this man hunts for you."

"Thank you for the offer, but I don't wish to leave," Elyna said. "Here I have things that can keep me busy, such as my gardens, and I have my powers. I would feel lost staying with you."

"I understand, and I know this Hand-D has

not been on your property yet, but it's too easy to find out where you live, and whether you have anyone guarding you. I would feel much better if you were with me, or your police friend could provide someone to stay here with you, since you have refused to let me assign one of my team."

"My police friend?" Elyna wondered how much Jemma knew about her feelings for Gabriel. Would she report the indiscretion to Aiden?

Jemma laughed. "I see you wonder what I know, and what I'll say to your Sorcerer King. Don't worry, Elyna—and no, I'm not reading your thoughts. I can feel your emotions when this Gabriel is near and it worries me, since Mai has tutored me in the laws and customs of your race. But I would never betray you to Aiden. I owe him for a favor granted me. The repayment does not extend to spying on his sister."

Elyna let out a sign of relief. She wasn't sure why she trusted Jemma on this, but perhaps it had to do with the stories she'd heard of Jemma running away from foster homes, and living on the streets of Seattle before her sister Larinda had begun to search for her. Then Larinda had died before they could meet. The estate Jemma had inherited hadn't made up for the losses she'd suffered or the shock it must have been when she learned she was not only Valens, but the fated leader of the race. Jemma knew what it was to be on your own, trusting only yourself.

"Jemma, do you know anything about what one should wear to go out with a man you want to impress? I'm hoping I can make him appreciate me before I have to explain what I am. And I may be banned from the Enclave and the world of the Fae when I do that. If that happens, I hope I can be as brave as you've been about all the changes in your life."

"Well, I am learning about fashion, or so my housekeeper assures me," Jemma said with a wry smile. "As for Aiden, let's not decide how he will react until we know what's going to happen with this Hand-D. Your brother cares, or he would not have asked me to return his favor instead of pulling you immediately back home. I don't think he will turn his back on you."

By the time Gabriel arrived, Elyna's bed was straining from the weight of the outfits she had tried on and discarded as too young, too old, too dressy, too casual—or that she couldn't remember what had made her buy them in the first place. With Jemma's help she settled on a sleeveless floral print dress with deep pink roses on a white background.

"You look—amazing," Gabriel said when she opened the front door.

"Do you have a lot of experience with girls dressing up to go out to dinner with you?" Elyna teased, though she had to admit she hoped he was going to say *no*.

Gabe shook his head. "I don't go out much, and when I do, it's usually with some of the other guys from the task force. But I had a friend who could morph from grunge rat to jaw-dropping gorgeous fairy princess when she needed to. Not that you usually look like a grunge rat," he added hastily.

"I'd love to meet her," Elyna said, smiling

at the description he'd used. Maybe he longed to be a prince charming in a fairy tale.

"She—she's not around anymore," Gabe said.

The sadness in Gabriel's voice told her that

"You lost touch with her?"

"No, she—she died."

Elyna felt the rage and grief spike through him. "I'm so sorry. I would never have mentioned it—"

"You didn't know," he said, before abruptly changing the subject. "So I hope you like pasta, and the most amazing dessert on the planet."

"Where are we going? I haven't been to many of the restaurants in the area."

He took her to a quiet and relaxing Italian

restaurant, owned by the family of friends. The chef was a master of the cuisine, equaling the chef of the Italian Fae ambassador. The flavors melded and blended for an experience she hadn't expected in the human world. At one point she almost blurted out something to that effect, but caught herself just in time. He was really good at his job as a police officer, and she was sure his natural curiosity would have been piqued, resulting in too many uncomfortable questions.

When Gabe opened his wallet to pay the check, a picture of a young woman tumbled out with his credit card. Elyna picked it up. She looked familiar. "Who's that?" she asked.

Gabe glanced down at the photo and was silent for several moments.

"Natalie," he finally said. "A—friend."

Elyna was shocked to realize where she had seen the picture before. "She was one of the victims," she said, and immediately cursed herself for being so tactless. How horrible. No wonder Gabe was so intent on catching the maniac. Natalie, who he called a friend, had been killed by Hand-D. Could she have been more than a friend?

"How do you know?" Gabe's voice was stiff and filled with pain.

"I remember seeing the pictures in the newspaper, and thinking how young they all looked. How sad it was that they didn't have the opportunity to do the things they must have dreamed about."

"She died because of me."

"How can you say that?" Elyna asked.

"She was only twenty-two—she came here to go to graduate school at the University in Denton. I knew her from high school—she and her dad lived in the same neighborhood as me and my family." He ran his fingers through his hair. "I can't explain what it was like for me. I had skipped a couple of grades, so I was much younger than everybody in my class. They all treated me like a little kid. But Natalie—she was always nice to me. We'd sit in her backyard, by the pool, and talk about books, and science, and just—life. She made me feel special."

His mouth twisted. "She was the first girl I ever kissed. We kind of had a thing, the summer before I went to college—but nobody else really knew about it. I was only sixteen, and she was eighteen—they would have thought it was weird, I guess."

He sighed. "It sounds sort of silly, now, but she really meant a lot to me. We drifted apart after we both went to college, and my mom divorced that stepdad, so we moved away. It was just a fluke, that my mom heard Natalie was coming to school here, and happened to mention it to me. It took me weeks to get the courage to track her down and ask her out." Sadness clouded his eyes. "The night she disappeared, we were supposed to meet for dinner, but something came up at work. I never saw her alive again."

As they walked out to the car, Elyna felt the need to comfort him. "It wasn't your fault, Gabe. You had to go to work. I'm sure Natalie would have understood that."

"I know in my head it was just one of those things that happens, but it doesn't make it easier to accept, or make me blame myself any less. I never told anyone before, but at the time, I really thought I was in love with her. In a twisted way, that was why I didn't jump at the chance to see her. I wanted to keep that feeling, those memories, and I was afraid that, after all the years I'd spent holding on to the fantasy, the reality wouldn't measure up. It's the reason I can't stop feeling guilty—maybe if we had gone to dinner, the bastard would never have gotten his hands on her. "

The silence between them grew. Gabe seemed lost in thoughts of the past, and Elyna searched for something to say to help.

He looked into her eyes. "I hate to ask, but

can you keep this a secret? No one knows that Natalie and I had a personal connection. It would have kept me off the task force. Of course when they investigated her death, they found my number in her phone records and talked to me, but as far as they knew we were just former neighbors. Since we hadn't seen each other in years, and I was at work at the time she disappeared, they only interviewed me once and that was it. But if they find out I had personal feelings for one of the victims, it could compromise the investigation. At best, I'd be kicked off the task force. And I need to bring this guy down."

She sat beside Gabriel in the car, watching him from the corner of her eye. Was he still in love with Natalie? Despite hearing about his feelings for the other girl, she found herself wanting to feel another kiss. Feel his arms around her. Did he know? Could he feel it? He glanced at her as he reached for the keys that dangled from the starter. Disappointment flooded through her. But he didn't start the motor. Instead he reached toward her, and her heart tumbled in her chest. She held her breath as he touched her gently, wrapping his fingers around her shoulder, drawing her toward him.

She screamed as pain ripped through her, and everything went dark.

* * * *

Elyna sat up in bed, trying to figure out where she was. Her head ached dully behind her eyes, and she vaguely remembered remnants of another vision. Glancing around, she realized she must be in Gabe's house. One of the guest rooms. Panicked, she threw back the covers. Relief swelled like an ocean wave when she realized she was still fully dressed. He hadn't discovered her wings.

"Elyna," Gabe called from the hallway, knocking lightly on the door. "Are you awake?"

When she didn't immediately answer, he carefully turned the knob and pushed open the door, a worried look on his face. When he saw her sit up, it turned to relief.

"Hi," he said. "You okay? You really worried me last night."

Last night? She'd been unconscious all night? "What—what happened?"

"You scared me half out of my mind. You

screamed, grabbing your head like you had to hold it on your shoulders, and a minute later you passed out. And you changed."

"Changed? I don't understand." She played dumb, trying to find out what she'd done. Had she lost control of her abilities? How much had he seen?

"I think you understand very well, Elyna. I don't understand what I saw, but the shape of your ears completely altered. How did that happen? I admit it was kind of cute but—weird."

She bit her lip, unable to answer without telling him who and what she really was.

"I admit it made me very curious, and I had to check you out. Is Elyna Faylinn even your real name? I had Records run a search and no one with that name seems to have lived around here before your aunt suddenly showed up and paid cash to buy the property where the nursery is located."

"You investigated me?" Elyna snapped. His eyes narrowed, and she held her breath, biting her lip. She knew he wouldn't believe her.

"I should have done it before," he said. "The only records of any Faylinns I could find were a driver's license for you and another for your aunt. No social security number, no credit cards. Who are you?"

"I left home a while back, and I'm using my aunt's last name." *Her human last name.*

"How did you get a driver's license without a birth certificate? Did you bribe someone to give it to you? Or did you use forged paperwork?"

This was getting too complex. How could

she possibly make him understand, believe that there was nothing suspicious—well, other than the fact she wasn't human. What would he think if she suddenly blurted out she was Fae? A Fairy. A *real* fairy. Would Aiden know the minute she told him? Mai had said her brother wasn't monitoring her thoughts. Elyna studied him, and then took a deep breath. If they were to have any chance of being together, she had to tell him sometime. He'd already seen her real appearance. Unless she trusted him with the truth, their relationship was over anyway. "I can't explain," she said. "I have to show you. Come into the backyard with me."

Gabe followed her, feeling confused and deceived. What could she possibly show him that would miraculously make him trust her?

The backyard looked just as dry and bleak as it had since the day he'd moved in. But as she walked away from him, toward the corner of the yard, he noticed tiny plants pushing through the dirt. They were spaced so far apart they looked like cactus in a black sand desert landscape, but they seemed to be arranged rather than random. How had he never noticed that before? Could she possibly have sneaked over sometime and done it to surprise him? It was beautiful, but it didn't change anything.

Elyna bent down, touching her hand to the ground. And—the stones in the ground started moving. By themselves. They edged the plants and formed a low retaining wall. Gabe watched, frozen, his mouth open. Then it got crazier.

The plants began to grow. Row after row of hedges. Flowers. Even trees, sprouting out of the ground like a time-lapse video, until they looked like they'd been there for years. Gabe's knees buckled and he sat down abruptly in a patio chair. This couldn't be real.

Turning, Elyna glanced at him, then walked quickly over to a single rectangle of dried-out grass sitting in the middle of the black dirt. Again, she bent and placed her hand on it. Gabriel watched, stunned, as the yard filled and became a rich emerald green. He opened his mouth, but nothing came out. She walked over to him, gave him a peck on his cheek, and then turned and walked back in the house.

Stumbling in after her, he sputtered, "What? How? Hell. How did you...? Hell, no one could do..." He turned and stared back out through the French doors, unable to believe his eyes. "What are you?"

Elyna took his hand and drew him to a chair at the table, urging him to sit down. She made a pot of coffee, feeling calmer than she'd thought she would. The delay gave him time to absorb what he had seen. Biting her lip, she set the cup in front of him, then sat down opposite. "The job you have, it teaches you—more than most—that people aren't always what they appear to be, right?"

He nodded slowly. "You're definitely not what you appear to be," he said.

"No," she said. "I belong to a race that you humans have relegated to folklore. We accepted this idea, and have remained hidden from human sight—"

Gabe shook his head. She knew he was unwilling to accept what he was hearing.

"I'm Fae, Gabe. More commonly called a fairy. We are not a group of tiny little beings that flit about the woods, but we are charged with protecting the environment. Finding a way to keep humans from destroying all that helps them survive."

"This is bull—"

"Then how did your yard transform in a matter of moments? You saw what I did. How would you explain it?"

"It's a trick. You did something to make it look like—I don't know, but it's *not* real."

She couldn't hold back a snicker of laughter. "What, you think I somehow dug out your yard and installed some system to make you think I could do this? Mirrors. I didn't use smoke, so…"

"Okay," he said. "I'm being ridiculous, but this—this—magic isn't real. Is it?"

"Very real, and a secret you can never reveal to anyone. Does it repulse you?" She was afraid her revelation would turn him from her, just as lies would have done.

"I don't know. I mean, do I think you're repulsive? No, but what can I say? I still can't believe what I saw or what you told me. I need some time to think about it."

Elyna nodded. She supposed that was the best she could expect, under the circumstances.

* * * *

Gabriel needed time to absorb what had happened at his house, but he needed to do something normal before he could even begin to try and understand it. He drove Elyna home and went to the station, arriving just as Dennis escorted two women to his desk. One of them was elderly, using a walker to scoot herself forward inch by inch. She was followed by a plain, exhausted-looking woman of about forty. The older one was hunched over, a fierce look on her prune-like face. Her eyes were dark and venomous, her lips curled down in a permanent frown.

"We checked back five years, ma'am," Dennis was saying. "Twice. No one named

Dorothy has died in this area of anything but natural causes. All of them in a hospital or nursing home, surrounded by their loved ones."

"You idiots," the woman snapped, pushing the walker out in front of her as she continued to move forward. "Dorothy. Dorothy Plunkett. My *sister.* I called you people an tole ya' there was something wrong. Tole ya' that hell hound had done somethin' to her. She stopped answering my letters." She glared at the man who stood before her. "Stupid," she spat. "You never went out ta look, did ya'? You never called me back. So here I am."

Dennis turned and just stared at the woman.

"When did you do this, Miz…"

"*Plunkett.* Velma Plunkett. 'Bout a year

ago. Went down to the grocer, made the call.
Then broke my hip. Had ta stay in bed, but Enid
checked, ya' never called back."

Dennis looked at Gabe, who shrugged.
He didn't remember anything about a call, but it
had probably never gotten to his desk.

"Well," Ms. Plunkett snapped. "Aren't you
gonna' git me a chair? 'Pect me to stand here all
day? Ain't never a gentleman around no more.
You young uns forget all about respect for your
betters."

Gabe was the first to move and swiftly
pulled a chair out from another desk, assisting the
woman as she slowly descended to a sitting
position. "There you go. Now, you were saying?"

"I don't wanna talk to you," she snarled,
turning toward Dennis. "You...fat guy, how long

you been workin' here?"

Dennis scratched his head then decided she was talking to him. "Been a detective for more than thirty years, Miz Plunkett."

"Well, you ain't a very good one. You people been runnin' around searchin' fer my nephew, Hubert. I read about it in the papers. You shudda called me back. I'd a tol' ya'. Now, what you gonna' do 'bout my sister?" she asked, spearing Dennis with her eyes.

"I'm sorry. We aren't looking for anyone named Hubert that I'm aware of."

"Course you are. That killer. Hubert. DOROTHY'S BOY. You people hard of hearin' or what? He's a demon born from hell. She had to bleed him reglar, tryin' to save his soul."

Gabe's adrenalin spiked. "You mean the

Hand-D Killer?" Gabe asked, losing his poker face.

"Stupid name. I said I don't wanna' talk to you, but yeah. That's who I mean. Hubert," she spat, snapping her jaws shut.

Gabe and Dennis sat, stunned, and listened to the tale of a horrifying childhood, and the twisted love that had grown a monster.

"We went out to the house. It's a damn shame the state it's in. So out of the way and overgrowed I wouldna' knowed it was there if I hadn't been before. But Dorothy loved that old shack. Too bad he ain't takin' care of it. The weeds are as tall as I am and the shutters are fallin' off. Locked up tighter than a tick, too. But he's been there."

A glance at Dennis's face told him his

partner was just as anxious to go to this shack as he was. Could this fiendish woman have given them the killer's hideout? And his identity? This might finally be the break they'd been looking for.

Chapter Eight

Elyna paced the living room as she went over the events that had led to her betrayal of the Fae. What would Aiden do? What would he think? She wondered if she should contact Mai, but was afraid the woman's loyalties would require reporting Elyna's indiscretion to her brother, even if she was sympathetic. A knock on the door interrupted her thoughts.

"Jemma! I'm so glad it's you. I was afraid—"

Jemma stepped into the room. "I came by to tell you the police have found out who the killer is. A man named Hubert Plunkett."

"What? They found out who Hand-D is? How? Are they sure?"

"Whoa. Take a breath. The report I got says that the man's aunt showed up unexpectedly and announced his identity and where he could be found. It's my understanding the taskforce is preparing to visit his house, but none of this is official. The police don't notify me when they plan a raid. Fortunately I have a friend or two who keep me informed. But you were stirred up before I told you any of this. Are you all right?"

Elyna explained what had happened at Gabe's the night before. "He's in shock. Doesn't know if he can accept what I am, but I guess I can't blame him. I wouldn't be surprised if he ends up hating me. He hardly said a word to me when he brought me home, and Aiden will find out I revealed the Fae, and…"

"At least he drove you home instead of just sneaking away like I did when Hawke told me about the Valens." Jemma smiled. "I doubt Gabriel hates you. You may have just confused him. I remember when I learned about the Valens. I did *not* want to believe in them." Jemma shook her head at the memory. "I kept ignoring it. Running away. Then I almost died. Hawke guided my rebirth to Phoenix."

"Wait. You said Gabe found out who the killer is and is going on a raid? He's going to arrest him? I need to be there. I can protect him."

"He'll be safe with my people, though he doesn't know members of the task force are

Valens," Jemma said. "You need to calm down and think about how you're going to explain all this to your brother. However, I'm pretty sure he'll understand, Elyna. He's been king for a very long time, and you are the baby sister he wishes to protect from all harm."

"How would you know? He's never done anything but boss me around, and then he insisted that I marry Raynard, who's a toad." She saw Jemma raise her eyebrows. "Not literally a toad," she amended. "I could never love him, but Aiden didn't care. He just wanted me to be the good little princess who did what she was told."

"He didn't send anyone to bring you back when you left," Jemma said.

"He sent Mai, and then you," Elyna challenged.

"Only after he knew you were in danger. That you had stumbled upon a murderer, and the madman would be looking for you. You're fortunate this Hubert person hasn't come here to your house."

"I can take care of myself."

"Perhaps, but I promised Aiden to guard you, and I keep my promises."

Elyna threw her hands into the air. "So, I can marry anyone he chooses, but he doesn't trust me to protect myself? He is the one who insisted I train with the warriors. What was the point, if my brother isn't going to trust me to use the skills I have?"

Jemma laughed, thinking about her own doubts as she learned to trust others. "It never hurts to have a friend who has your back, Elyna.

Perhaps your Gabriel doesn't know what you can do, and may still think this is all something he's imagined. But it's not, and your bother knows this. You are Fae and I am Valens, facts that humans have a hard time accepting. This is why we hold our secrets and caution our wards against revealing the truth. Now we have to decide how to ensure the killer is captured, and no one else is harmed."

* * * *

The police entered the house just as though they believed Plunkett was there. The SWAT team covered every exit; then, taking the ram, they knocked the front and back doors open at precisely the same time. It only took a few minutes to confirm nothing alive occupied the small rooms.

"Okay, boys. Out. Thanks. We want Bailey and his team to clean this place up without a bunch of clumsy-footed SWAT do-gooders getting in the way." Gabe looked around as the men left. The dark rooms were full of debris. The house was going to give them everything they needed to put Hubert "Hand-D" Plunkett away for good—hopefully give him the needle. He walked carefully into the front room, feeling the horror all around him.

He'd expected the blood, and maybe even the trophies, but he still hadn't realized the effect this place would have on him. Years of candle wax pooled on every surface in the living room. Crosses of every size and description were nailed to the walls. The iron-rich smell of dried blood filled his nostrils, mixed with the baser scents of death. Skeletons and rotting carcasses of animals littered the floor.

Slowly Gabe moved down the hallway toward the bedroom where the women had been tortured. The SWAT leader had done a brief walk-through, coming back pale and shaken. Gabe knew it would be bad.

Dennis came out of the room. "Don't. You don't need to go in there. Gabe, he's got pictures of all of them plastered like wallpaper. He musta taken the photos as he went through each step when he tortured them. You don't need to see Natalie looking at you like that from the walls."

Gabe stopped, looking at his partner. "You knew?"

"It's not surprising you never recognized me. You were in shock over her death. I poked around your living room while old man Donnely interviewed you. Felt like something was off, the way you reacted. You alibied out, so we dismissed you as a suspect, but when the guy killed again, I did a little more digging into your past. Talked to her dad's pool boy, found out about your high school romance. When you showed up as a rookie, I kept an eye on you. Figured out pretty quick you weren't the killer, and you had the dedication to work the task force. So I kept my mouth shut about you and her. When you asked the Chief for the assignment, I backed you up. After all, we need your special skills." Dennis shrugged.

Gabe walked forward, steeling himself for what lay beyond his partner. "Move. I need to see for myself."

Dennis stepped aside and waited as Gabriel entered the room. Faces, in all stages of fear and pain, stared down from the walls. Gabe walked the perimeter of the room, trying to prepare himself for what he'd already seen was over the bed. All of them were there. Gabe finally looked up at the face above the headboard. Natalie's pictures took up the center space. He ran from the house to throw up, then cursed Dorothy Plunkett for the madman she'd created.

Chapter Nine

Dennis called Elyna, asking her to come to Gabe's. He didn't specifically say why, but his voice held a note of urgency. When she landed under the trees by the road, she straightened her clothing and walked up the drive to the door. The older man let her into the house. Gabe was pacing back and forth in his office, and she didn't need any special powers to sense the waves of pain he radiated.

"What happened, Dennis? Why is he acting like this?"

"We found Hand-D's hideout. Did Gabe

tell you about Natalie?"

Elyna nodded.

"Gabe thought he was prepared, but when he saw the bastard's pictures of her..." Dennis broke off, running his hands through his hair. "I should never have let him work this case—not after I found out he was connected to one of the victims. No one can take seeing someone they cared about like that."

Elyna's hand went to her mouth. She couldn't imagine having to face those horrific images.

Dennis looked at her pleadingly. "I can't get through to him, Elyna. Could you try? He seems to—well, you two seem to have a connection. I thought maybe..."

Startled, she looked at the older man. "I

don't know if I can do anything, but I can try," she said. She went quietly into the office, considering the tools available to the Fae. Her personal gifts: growth, flight, shielding. None of those would help. There were others, things she had been taught as a child that she could call upon, but there had never been a need to do so, and she was afraid she would fail should she attempt to use them. "Leave him with me," she said, wondering if it was a mistake. "I'll see what I can do."

She had never tried the Fae power of easing a soul. She had learned the technique, but usually the healers practiced this art. She looked over at Gabriel, who was still pacing. She called to him, but he either didn't hear, or he ignored her. Praying she had the skill, and the rite would work on a normal human, she stood and walked toward the man she had come to love.

Reaching out, she took his arm. He struggled briefly to twist away, but she was strong and held on. Drawing his lean, muscular body toward her, she wrapped him in her arms and held on until he stopped fighting. Quickly moving to cup his face in her hands, she drew her fingertips across his temples, massaging lightly. Placing her ear to his heart, she said the words she had been taught and prayed all the feelings he was experiencing would wash over her, flow through her, and give him relief.

The pain buckled her knees as it entered her and passed through. She glimpsed pictures of what he had seen. She wanted to stop, push the images away, beg for relief. Yet this desire only proved the mantra was working. She held on as the horror invaded her body and slowly washed away into the night. Tears rolled down her face, the tears he could not shed. His anger, as it stole through her, threatened to shatter her heart. She held on until he began to calm.

Slowly, his frantic heartbeat eased, and she could feel the tension ebbing from his shoulders. Taking his hand, she led him into the bedroom and put him to bed. She took off his shoes and drew the covers over him, watching as he fell into a deep, dreamless sleep.

He would not remember what she had shared with him. He would remember how badly he had been affected, but the emotional intensity would be gone. When he returned to work, he would be able to read and write the reports, see the photos, and continue doing the job he loved. She sat with him until morning light peeked thought the curtains, and then quietly left the house and returned home. He couldn't find her there when he woke. Now all she could do was wait to see if he would forgive her for being what she was—and for hiding it from him. See if he would want her back in his life.

* * * *

He was running late, surprised at how well he had slept. He wondered if Elyna sitting by his bed, hand on his heart, had been a dream? She had seemed so real, but when he had gotten up she was nowhere in the house. There was no evidence she had been there at all. He took a quick shower and fixed a cup of coffee for the road, then rushed to the car. There would be a follow-up concerning the failed raid. Plans to be made on next steps. But the odds had changed—they knew who the monster was and that would give them the opportunity they needed to find him.

Gabe climbed into the driver's seat, his mind still on the case. The cold steel of the knife at his throat took him completely by surprise. Looking in the rearview mirror, he saw the face of a madman. The Hand-D Killer.

"Drive," the man growled.

Fury washed over Gabe. This was the man who had tortured and killed Natalie. Gabe wanted to grab the knife and carve the bastard into tiny pieces. But all he could do was drive to wherever this guy wanted to take him. His heart pounded in his chest. At Hand-D's direction, he turned onto a dirt road, the car jolting over deep ruts. The freak was taking him to some farmhouse or barn back away from the main thoroughfares. When they stopped, he was going to kill this guy. Just one little slip and Hand-D would be dead.

Gabriel pulled up to a dilapidated shanty similar to the one the team had raided, but miles from that location. Hand-D slid out after Gabriel and, with the knife resting against the center of Gabe's back, directed him where to go.

"You're sick," Gabriel spat. "Sick and useless."

Plunkett's voice was devoid of emotion. "Look who's talking. I'd say you're the useless one. I'm gonna enjoy killing you. I saw you with the girl from the nursery. Hope maybe she cares enough to feel sad you're dead. I'll get to her when her friend leaves after your funeral."

"You stay away from her, you freak," Gabriel growled, turning toward the killer.

"What you gonna do? Stupid. I'll drop you before you take one step. Turn around. In the house."

"I mean it, Hubert. You touch one hair on her head and you're a dead man."

"Sissy cop, whining about your whore. It's a shame I won't get to kill her first. Make you watch. I think it would be much more fun having you watch her die."

Gabe knew it was stupid to argue, but he couldn't stop.

"You slime. Is your mamma, Dorothy,

telling you what to do? Does she tell her little boy

how bad he is? Punish him when he's been

naughty?"

"NOOOO."

Hubert was becoming more and more

agitated. Gabe had to be careful. He knew the

man was dangerous, no matter how insane he

might be. He was strong, and even a weakling is

dangerous with a knife. And he was clever—it

had taken two years to learn enough about him to

begin an honest search effort. But taunting him

was the only prayer Gabe had that the man would

make the one mistake he could take advantage

of.

* * * *

Gabriel watched the killer walk about the

room, setting out candles, crosses, preparing it just as he had the room where the women had been tortured in the house they had raided. His heart tripped and hammered, but he fought to remain calm. He knew the worst this man could do. He had seen the bodies. His stomach rolled as he realized he was here, in the same position. He knew what was coming. There was only one question. When?

He forced himself to think. In all the mountains of data he'd analyzed there must be a clue to how to deal with Hand-D. How to stay alive. He knew he had to remain calm. Find a way to use the information.

Weak. Angry. Hurting. He struggled to clear his mind, but failed as the killer stood over him. "You filth," Gabe rasped. "You killed your mother, all those women. For what? Does it make you feel like a big man?"

Hubert just stood, watching, sharpening his knife. "You'll see what a big man I am when I get your doxy and bring her here. You'll watch her die."

"You're nothing. Less than nothing. And you're the one who will die," Gabriel spat.

* * * *

"Elyna, I'm sorry. We've looked everywhere. I'm afraid—"

"NO." Elyna clutched the phone receiver. "He's still alive. I know it. Dennis, you can't stop searching."

"We won't. We haven't. As long as he's

missing, we'll keep looking. But you need to understand, the longer he's missing—well, in case—"

"I know you're trying to prepare me for the worst, but he's alive." She sighed. She didn't want to fight with this man. He was a friend of Gabriel's and wanted to find him almost as much as she did.

"Yeah. Okay. I'll call you if—no, when—we find him."

Hanging up, she knew it was up to her. The police had found Hand-D's car down the street from Gabe's house, and were already sure he was dead. There was nothing she could say that would change their minds. They had put the man's picture in the paper, and would continue to look, but it would be half-hearted.

The moon had set, but her night vision allowed her to see for miles. As the air current lifted her, she flew in the direction her heart pulled her. She would find him—alive.

Heartbroken, exhausted, she circled one final house before landing, and tucked her wings away. The sun was rising, the clouds already touched by the violets and vibrant golden pinks of dawn. It shamed her to notice the early morning beauty. Distracted by guilt, it took her a moment to realize someone was there, as a door opened and he stepped into the dark yard. Silently she crept closer until she was sure the man was Hubert Plunkett, the Hand-D Killer. He had walked to a picnic table where he now sat washing items in a small tub in front of him. Gabriel's gun lay on the table within reach. She considered her approach, what she would do.

She had to disable the killer. Making her

decision, she rose on silent wings, high into the

sky, and plunged toward him in a surprise attack.

Moments before striking, she spread her

wings to act as a brake, and swung her body

forward, feet positioned to strike. With the speed

of a striking snake, he snatched up the gun and

fired wildly. Pain ripped through her right wing

and she swirled out of control, her wing hanging

uselessly, the ground rushing toward her. Her

body slammed into it, and everything went dark.

She woke, gagging, as the man knelt over

her and forced liquid into her throat. She

struggled to spit it out, but only succeeded in

choking. She gasped and tried to lift her arm to

push the bottle away. Pain shot though her,

broken bones in her wrist grinding together. She passed out again.

"Elyna. Elyna. Wake up." Gabriel's voice, hoarse and gravelly, came from above her. "Are you all right? *Elyna*."

She lay on the dirt-covered floor, unable to move anything except her eyes. Rolling them upward, she could barely see the edge of the bed where Gabriel appeared to be tied to the bedpost. Unable to speak, she could give him no assurance she was alive. She scanned what she could of the room. Light leaked through the dirty windows, so it was daytime, but she had no idea what day. Whatever the killer had given her had destroyed her sense of time, but did nothing to ease the pain where he'd shot her.

Glancing down her body, she tried to

determine if she was tied up, or if the drug she had ingested was the only thing restraining her. No ropes. Her captor must believe she would be incapacitated for some time, yet even now, beyond the pain, she could feel tingling in her hands and feet as they began to awaken from their enforced paralysis. A muffled voice and the slamming of a door drew her attention.

"Get in there, you sniveling idiot. Get her off that floor and tie her to the chair."

"You shot the angel. You changed her to Dorothy. You shot the angel."

"Stupid fool. That was not an angel. She's the one you've been waiting for. MOVE."

Shocked, Elyna realized that Plunkett was the only person entering the bedroom, and he was arguing with himself. His voice took on a higher pitch as it berated him, as if it belonged to someone else.

"If I didn't need you to finish this, I'd kill you right now."

She could hear the killer babbling unintelligible words, his footsteps coming closer. "Stay away from her, you filth," Gabriel yelled hoarsely.

"And if I don't? You think you can stop me from doing anything I want?" Hand-D's voice sneered. "Look at you. You can hardly move. Even if you could, you're no match for me. What are you going to do?" Hubert moved to the side of the bed and held his knife to Gabriel's neck, the blade gleaming in the dim light. "Stupid fool," he said.

Elyna tried to move, take the killer by

surprise, but the white-hot pain of the bullet wound made her gasp involuntarily. He turned toward her.

"You weren't fooling me," he said. "I knew you were awake. You're another helpless, stupid fool. You can hardly move, and there's no chance you can untie this freak," Hand-D challenged.

"You're right," she answered. "I can't untie him. You broke my arm. But I won't let you harm him, no matter what it takes." She slowly pushed herself up as the killer watched. Forcing herself to ignore the pain, she reached out with her good arm, and placed her hand on Gabriel's shoulder.

Hand-D began to draw the knife lightly across Gabriel's neck. Blood beaded along the incision.

"NO. Please," she begged. "Stop. Let me have a moment, one last kiss." She didn't fight the tears forming in her eyes. Desperately, she searched her mind for something to end this horror.

He stopped, removing the knife, and stared at her across the bed. "Oh, yes, please take a moment to say goodbye," he scoffed. "It will be such a pretty sight. I can feel your terror rising, so I don't mind taking another moment or two before I kill him."

She used her hand on Gabe's shoulder to pull herself up to sit on the edge of the bed, too weak to do it alone. Carefully she bent forward, placing a gentle kiss on Gabriel's lips. Suddenly she felt it... Gabriel's cut began to seal. She could feel the energy course from her into him.

She watched as he looked at her, questioning, and then he seemed to understand. "Fly away, my love," she said. "Believe, and fly away."

Gabriel's body rippled and shimmered. Hand-D plunged forward, the knife slicing through the air, but Gabriel was no longer lying on the mattress. A powerful eagle rose from the bed, talons ripping at the killer's face and neck.

Hubert screamed and dropped the knife, trying to protect his face. He stumbled back and fell, his head hitting the edge of a nightstand. He dropped to the floor, stunned, eyes open and staring off in the distance, unseeing.

Gabriel flew back to the bed. Elyna laid her hand on his head and prayed for him to return to his natural form. The eagle shimmered once more, and became Gabe. After staring down at his body for a second, he scooped up Plunkett's knife from the floor, and cut lengths of rope from his own bonds to tie Plunkett's hands behind his back.

"You were supposed to fly away," Elyna shouted. "Mother of the Fae, you were supposed to fly away." Then she was in his arms, crying, thanking all the powers he was safe.

He held her tightly, careful not to crush her injured arm, until her tears slowed. Gently he pushed away. "I need to get Dennis out here. Have him take care of this trash." He picked up the killer's knife, and his own gun from the nightstand. Then he bound Plunkett's legs so that he couldn't get away.

Gabriel ran outside to his car, grabbing his portable radio from the glove compartment, calling in the troops.

* * * *

Dennis looked at the rope burns on his partner's wrist. "So, Houdini, what really happened out there?"

"Just like I told you and the others. I got loose."

"Sure. So ya' just stood up and he passed out."

"Dennis, leave Gabe alone. He's got his story, and you can't change it," Elyna said. She looked at Gabriel, her eyes glistening with humor. "We have to leave. We have an appointment with my brother, and we don't want to be late."

Dennis arched an eyebrow, wondering about the appointment, but Gabe had been adamant in his resolve not to talk about the abduction, how Elyna had found him, or anything to do with the girl's family. He didn't see them step out of the building and pass through a magical passage that delivered them to Ireland moments later.

Thunder rolled over the Enclave. Lightning danced, numerous strikes hitting the ground. "Aiden's angry."

"We aren't even in the building yet. How do you know?" Gabriel looked puzzled.

"His gift." Elyna swept her hand toward the sky. "Others can mimic a small portion of his might, but the power to make the air dance and the sky roar this way belongs to him."

Gabriel looked up at the dark, rolling clouds, wondering what else there was to learn about these people.

Inside the halls, the Council chamber was filled to capacity, but the sea of Fae parted as they passed. Aiden stood in front of the dais clothed in his robes of state, his staff glowing.

Gabriel stepped up, trying to shield Elyna. "Before you—"

"*Sit* down." Aiden's frosty glare sent a chill through the air. "I will deal with you later. Elyna, daughter of the Fae, stand before me." His words carried an arctic cold.

"My King." Elyna bowed slightly, determined not to tremble as she awaited his judgment. She straightened her back, standing proud before the Fae leader.

"You come for judgment. What have you to say?"

Taking a deep breath, she said, "I meant no disrespect in leaving when you demanded I marry Raynard, but I had to follow my heart and discover my fate. Nothing more can be said." Would that mean anything to Aiden? He was her brother and she knew he loved her, but he was also the Sorcerer King and could not allow his people to think he might excuse her when he would not do so with another.

"You do not defend this man who stands at your side?"

"My defense would be a repetition of what you have already heard. The man is meant for me and I for him. He is the man who will stand beside me for all of his days, and he is a great warrior who has fought for me and won against immeasurable odds. I am not ashamed to be a part of his life."

Aiden softened. "Sister, you have seen so much darkness, yet you still glow with light. You have faced the worst of mankind, and can see beyond this horror."

"I have someone beside me who gives me strength. I will *not* regret losing my powers as payment, should that be your judgment."

Aiden waived his hand in dismissal. "You will suffer no further loss at my hand."

Tears poured from her eyes and she began to shake as the meaning of his words penetrated. "I don't know what to say. I'm not worthy—"

"You are, but he may not be," Aiden said, pointing his finger, then crooking it, calling Gabriel forward. "Let me hear your words. Elyna has much faith in you, human. Faith enough to have shared a gift with you."

Elyna's returning fear almost took her to her knees. Aiden could forbid Gabe from ever seeing her again, a ruling that had no recourse. Or he could force her to marry the one he had chosen for her. Worse, he could force her to watch as Gabriel grew old and became lost to her, removing Gabe's memory of her and the love they shared.

Gabriel stepped forward, hoping the nervousness he felt didn't show. The man standing in front of him emanated overwhelming power. "Elyna shared," he agreed. Pulling himself up to full height he shot back, "That's not against your rules, is it?"

Aiden's laughter rang through the air.

"You have a hard time being humble, don't you? No, sharing the gift to save a life is not against our laws. However, humans usually don't have the stamina to allow them to fight as you did. Your lady may be right, you could be a warrior."

He couldn't suppress the cocky grin. "Thank you."

"However, in sharing, she has changed things in this universe. Your binding must be blessed. I do so here. Now, you must learn to be humble in the presence of your ruler."

"What?" Gabe looked at Elyna for an explanation.

Elyna's looked stunned as the import of Aiden's words struck her.

Gabriel continued to look from Elyna to Aiden. Confusion written across his face, he opened his mouth.

Aiden smiled at him. "Gabriel, you are now a son of the Fae. You shall have the gift of love and long life. You may again use the power your mate has granted you, should the need arise. Take care in its application. I invite you to return soon and learn control."

"Elyna, in granting the gift to this man, you found a power long forgotten. This will be only the beginning of the discovery of the powers you bear. I appoint you one of the seven guardians. Together you and your bond-mate shall protect the Northern New Earth. You will have the power of earthfire and summerstorm. Warrior Gabriel, you will protect your bond-mate and be granted the movement of time and place to help her."

Elyna gaped in stunned silence. Nothing

had prepared her for the gifts Aiden offered.

They spent the day at her childhood home. Gabriel met all the members of the family who were now his. Mind reeling as he tried to remember all the names and faces, he sat in a corner watching the flurry of activity.

Elyna soon joined him, throwing her arms around his neck, trailing kisses along his jaw as he used his new power to transport them back to their home, away from the prying eyes of her family.